ACROSS COBBLED ALLEYS

A Coming of Age Tale

Written By Ty R. Jansma

Holy Oak Publishing, 2015

Dear Reader,

Thank you for taking time out of your busy lives to read this book. Over the past three years, I've found a distinctive voice as a writer. The book that you see before your eyes today has undergone many transformations and alterations on its journey to becoming this final product.

My audience, while in the midst of the creation of this book, was solely internal. It's an honor to finally make this an **external** production that I can share with you. Additionally, though many characters may resemble people you might know, characters are based solely on my imagination and derived through hundreds of hours of dedicated thought, heavily revised and continually recreated. Any similarity to real persons is unintentional. Thank you from the bottom of my heart for helping me to accomplish one of my greatest dreams.

Many Blessings,
Ty Jansma

Special Thanks to:

My mother for always challenging me to make this book better and for believing in me before the first page was even written. My good friend Andy for his dedication to the craft of writing and for his outstanding sense of humor. To Hannah, Holly and Dad for your support and love in all that I do. It keeps me going forward. To my sampling readers who read excerpts and tore them apart with and for me (you know who you are), and countless others thank you for being a part of my greatest dream coming to fruition. To my students, past and present, believe big! Without belief you can be washed away with the tides. Find your calling, latch onto it and seek it with all of your heart.

Ty Jansma

Travels

I've always had a strange infatuation with travel. Whenever the opportunity has arisen, I have tried my best to seize it and to go. I would encourage you, from the bottom of my heart, to do the same. The creation of this book has seen many cities. I based many of the individual stories that make up the tapestry of ACA about the cities I have traversed throughout the past few years of my life.

<u>Cities where this book truly took shape:</u>

- Santa Rosa Beach, Florida
- Atlanta, Georgia
- Nashville, Tennessee
- Lookout Mountain, Tennessee
- Grand Rapids, Michigan
- Bluffton, South Carolina
- Beaufort, South Carolina
- Birmingham, Alabama

If the opportunity arises to travel somewhere your heart desires, I urge you to go. Sometimes you'll have to create your own opportunity. That's not the worst way to go either. Seek and you will surely find.

All my love,

Ty

Across Cobbled Alleys

Chapter 1

It was a full harvest moon in Michigan that night. The man in the moon stood out indescribably, outlined by a flickering white light that illuminated the streets where I watched my youth fade away forevermore. The night was still; there was a keen sense of peace amongst the blackness. Like a lightning bolt, out of nowhere my phone vibrated and buzzed annoyingly in my khaki short pocket. I reluctantly answered it, not wanting to break the silence of the night, only to hear my best friend's voice, sounding much more exasperated than usual. He minced no words, and got straight to the point.

"I've got to get out of here. I keep seeing her face, man. Every last place I go, there she is. There they are— her and that curly headed asshole. I'm falling on my sword here man, I know I probably sound weak as hell, but I have to go. Grab your suitcase. I'm heading that way to pick you up. The holy boy road beckons. It beckons more than ever has a road beckoned," he said without taking a breath. Alec and I had many road trips under our belts. Together we had traveled from coast to coast exploring and searching for purpose. We both felt better equipped for living after an insanely last minute excursion. Without notice, the phone line clicked without time for a proper response.

The tall, lanky shadow of Alec Stone burst upon my

6

driveway precisely seventeen minutes later. His bushy brown hair, a bit too short on the sides and a pinch too long on top, jostled and jumped in the breeze upon exiting his aged Honda Civic. His clothes were well worn, signs of good use with plentiful memories attached, and he smiled with a dimple deep in his left cheek smirk. We stood nearly the same height and were of a similar weight, but our physical similarities stopped there. My hair, sand grain in color in contrast with his chocolate espresso shade, was much longer than his and always worn to the side over my forehead. I tended to care about my appearance more than I should have, opting for bright colors or unique patterned attire from various preppy brands. On this given evening, I wore above the knee khaki shorts and a Carolina blue Vineyard Vines tee shirt.

"Stone, where do we *have* to go? I know it's annoying seeing her all around here everywhere over and over again. Where'd you see her this time?" I asked all too logically, brushing hair off of my brow, and pondering what his current crisis was.

"Turner, does it really matter where I saw her? I see her when I'm awake and when I'm asleep. Every time I'm driving around town and I see a park, I think of the nights we'd lay under the stars lost in one another. Every time I pass our favorite restaurants or concert venues, I think of our outings and anniversaries and celebrations. I can't just go around seeing the same damn thing day after day with all of the memories of her attached. There are innumerable other things and places I want to see. We need to get out Rochester and you know it. This past year has been hell. On top of everything with Callie, my job sucks. My love life doesn't exist. I have no money to speak of. I need to see and do something else. And it came to me tonight like an albatross—when my rubber roadrunner wheels hit the pavement of the open road, I always seem to find some semblance of purpose," he cooed.

His emotional upheaval was all too apparent. He seemed unable to convey where he wanted to go, but I figured he didn't actually know the answer yet.

"I know the memories can hang onto the branches of trees, seeming like they're hanging above everything you do. Trust me, I've felt it. I remember all too distinctly how shitty a feeling it is. If I have to hear from Jez one more time, I swear I'll go insane. Is she texting you again? What could she even want from you at this point?"

"No clue. She's still messing with me. She still texts me now and again to wish me well and other shit that I would rather hear from any other person on the planet. Does she really think I want her to contact me like that? I'm not long for sticking around here. I think my heart is broken beyond repair," he whimpered.

"Maybe she contacts you because she feels bad about what she did. I know breakups hurts. Especially when you put everything you have into it and it doesn't pan out the way you expect. I am

8

really sorry man," I patted his shoulder.

"It's all good," he said shrugging, impossible to believe.

"No, it's not, but I understand. You'll make it through this, Alec," I said empathically.

Shifting gears, my mind began to wonder where Alec thought we might up and flock to in the middle of the night with no good plan in sight.

"Stone, even if we left right now, riddle me this: where would we go? Where is it that we could go with no prior notice whatsoever?" I asked. His face conveyed a sarcastic sense of relief.

"That's the easiest question you've posed all day. Where would the Lord want us to go? We will put the car in drive and head due south. As far South as we can get."

"Will you for one moment act sane? Where the hell would we *really* go?" I asked adamantly. Saying let's go south was about as general as one could be.

His eyes lit up like a circus and his hands flailed in the air, shaking and pleading for understanding.

"That's the problem, Turner. Everybody spends so much time lost in their logic—always trying to reason and precisely define answers. Life is not definable, not ever. Our path will not simply find us. We must seek it. And so we shall seek. Are you with me?"

He was profound and accurate; maybe I was overthinking the whole thing again. Being gone, away, free—that wouldn't be so extraordinarily horrific would it?

Nothing was out of the ordinary when it came to the great Alec Stone. He was persistent and adamant, but generally not to the point of being manipulative. We clicked instantaneously upon meeting several years earlier in the 9th grade at Worthington Academy, a small private school tucked in the suburbs of Rochester, Michigan. He was confident even then, despite being all of five foot three inches tall.

Looking at Alec Stone, philosophical and frustrated to the point of tugging at his own hair the question begged itself in my mind... why should I stay? Why, after all the agony of the last few years of my life, would I ever want to stay? I had a new job that I enjoyed as a local basketball coach and a wonderfully close-knit family, but in the pits of the last year, even the things I loved couldn't resolve my struggle. It all became clear, like a lightning bug casting its precious light on an ink black night, Alec Stone might have a remedy for the haze. I always wanted to go. The urgency just began to take precedent.

"So, are you truly down for leaving? Like sincerely, ready to go right this moment, leave this whole cluster behind us?" He asked with intrigue.

"I can't believe I'm saying this, but let's do it. Maybe we could head for Florida where I used to stay as a kid and rent a condo or something. Do you have any money saved?"

"Florida's nice. I don't want to have a destination. Let's just go. I

10

have my Dad's American Express card and a suitcase in the trunk with all my stuff," he quickly replied.

Breathing heavily, with sudden anticipation, I released my inhibitions. "Let's do this. This is absolutely insane man, but I need it too. Let's go!"

Moments later, we came barreling down the front stairs with backpacks slung over our slumped shoulders and suitcases in hand. We were approaching the car when headlights cast up the winding driveway to my home. It was the Jeep driven by my 20-year-old sister, Desi. Desi exited the vehicle and smiled her sunshiny smile.

"Where are you guys going with all that stuff?" she asked inquisitively. She was good natured, and read people very well. Stone had a jolly-smacked grin across his face and set down the twenty-four pack of Pabst Blue Ribbon beer slung under his arm. "My dear Desi, your brother and I are embarking on an adventure to the great south."

"So we decided definitively on that?" I laughed.

"I believe we did," Stone chuckled.

"You know how the past year or so has been tough, right?" He asked rhetorically. "Well, I need to spend some time at the beach. I need to taste the ocean and feel the sunshine burning into my skin," he smiled while shaking his head to and fro.

"You're just going to up and go south? And in the middle of the freaking night? That's a little last minute, isn't it?" Desi asked.

"Why the hell not?" Stone said, jumping around.

She rolled her eyes and turned toward me.

She wasn't the epitome of responsibility, but she looked concerned and curious.

"Turner, I know why Alec would wanna leave, but why the hell would you want to? You just landed that coaching job you've been wanting. It doesn't really make a lot of sense to abandon that opportunity," her voice trailed off hollowly.

"I know it might not make sense on paper, but I think Stone might be on to something right now. I've never needed something so bad as to be a best friend, to be an adventurer and to break free from this monotony. This life—it's not for me. Maybe it's for everybody else, but it just doesn't do it for me. I need to squeeze more out of my life," I said passionately.

She marinated on my thoughts.

"Me too, I understand it's frustrating but it's quite a leap to just leave on such a whim. Are you sure about this?"

"Absolutely," I replied, even though everyone present knew I wasn't sure at all.

She looked back with the innocence of a child.

"Okay, I trust you," she smiled and paused looking into the spooky night sky.

"Do you think I could come too? I mean I'm sick of things here at home too. I could use a change up," she mumbled.

"Really? You'd want to come on a whim like this? I don't know if

12

that would be smart," I began to say, realizing how hollow my words sounded.

In classic big brother, little sister fashion, she retorted back quickly.

"Well, you're going. Why can't I?"

"Alec, what do you think?" I asked.

"I think why not? One more person could make the road all the more interesting. Doesn't your boyfriend live in Birmingham, Alabama anyway? When's the last time you saw him?" He asked.

"Yeah, I wouldn't call him my boyfriend or whatever, but this guy I know pretty well lives there. I saw him a few months ago I guess. I am sure we could probably stay with him for a night or two."

"Even better," Stone shouted happily.

Desi ran upstairs, stuffed her bohemian clothes into a Louis Vuitton bag, and before we knew it, she was back and ready to depart south, hopefully toward her on again, off again lover, James Ryan.

"Did you tell mom and dad?" Desi probed.

"I didn't want to bother them with it. It's the middle of the night. I told them earlier I might spend a few days at the cottage up north. That could be work as a cover for now at least," I said.

"That works. I'll call them from the road. No sense in getting them all worked up at this hour," she replied.

Bags piled upon more bags in my old BMW 325i sedan, we

set out for something purposeful; perhaps we only set out on a wild haired adventure in search of peace. All the same, three wanderers turned on their headlights and the road opened wide as the skies. "There's something here, old friend," I said to Alec peacefully as the engine roared. "And I have a strong feeling we will soon find it."

He beamed with an organic smile for the first time in far too long, glancing over while grabbing the wheel tightly with one hand. And with that, we left Michigan behind.

Across Cobbled Alleys

Chapter 2

The car roared onward striking bump after bump on the weather worn Michigan highway. The temperature was dropping dramatically and dry heat blew in our faces from the car vents.

" I need to find something so indescribably purposeful that I actually feel rejuvenation down in the deepest stretches of my bones. I need to taste it, to breathe it, to haphazardly chase it until my insides and my brains is in perfect harmony once again," Stone announced poetically.

Alec Stone was always rifling off contradictory rants—rants that made very little sense but had a dramatic impact on the listener regardless. I smiled and didn't respond. Locating his purpose was all about taking action really. We both knew that. It wasn't as much looking for a specific thing as it was about finding an ideology that spoke to his heart. Finding something so poignant that he could forget Callie, his battle with brokenness, and his insurmountable financial struggles. He needed to find a feeling of security and success simultaneously rippling through the current of boiling blood on his insides. At 22 years old, penniless, single, and stuck in an awkward grey between child and adult, yet much closer to fully fledged adult than child, many things don't seem to make sense. When you're an 11-year-old kid, you think for the entire world that when you are 22, your life will be on the path you wished for it to be on and each and every component would be in its perfect place. Fast-forward to 22 and it's easy to begin to wonder if you'll know anything more at 44 or if that's just a hoax, too.

As the rain began to hit heavily on our windshield, Alec popped open a cold beer while slumping down in the passenger seat. It always scared me when he drank in the car, but there was no talking sense to his stubborn side.

"I've felt like giving up so badly lately, man. I just feel stuck. Not just an ordinary kind of stuck in a rut, down in the dumps, you know? Like I'm in the most uncomfortable place I have been in in my entire life that I cannot profoundly describe. Life without love is damned lonely," he shook his head in disgust with his own mortal life.

"Isn't it funny that when we start to give up, the most incredible and similarly horrifying things can happen? Nothing is off the table any longer, we say whatever comes to our mind, we do not edit or minimize our thoughts, and sometimes we spew off until our mouth run off?" His pontification was apparent.

"There's got to be more to this existence than meets the eye. The season is ripe with opportunity for blessed new encounters. I put a direct emphasis on the word *new*.

I continued, "You can't give up, though. Regardless of the burden, you can't throw in the towel on life."

"Turner, every time I desire something beyond my own ability to comprehend it, it falls short. Yet, when my faith in a situation is lowly, suddenly, it flourishes and takes on legs! God seems to forget me sometimes. Especially when it comes to love," he lamented.

Stone was referencing his former flame, Callie Peters. She was by all accounts his "first love," whom I had introduced him to during the first moments of college. Callie was a freckle-faced blond, tall and rail thing, nothing to look at really but still, beautiful in her own simplicity. Truly, I did not think their love would blossom—they were opposite people simply in the same place—a small, Christian college in the suburbs of the cottage lined houses of Grand Rapids, Michigan—so surely, true to token form, their love connection took off at the speed of light. They were carried by the winds of love, aloft to an oblivion-like state. It is the most euphoric experience of our earthly existence, which tickles your fingertips until the nerve endings drop. That is, until they cannot drop any longer.

Just after Callie and Alec experienced the conundrum that is *love*, I walked down a similar plank at a similar time in a nearby place. Jez entered my life unpredictably, when there was no rhyme or reason for it. 14-karat gold streaks highlighting her hair and hazel eyes big as almonds, she stood five foot six inches and had an average square bodied figure, with identifiable curves and creamy tan skin.

"Do you ever think about Jez, Turner?" Alec asked, shifting his focus temporarily to me.

"I try not to. She comes up from time to time. You know, I can't help thinking about how it ended when I'm sad at night sometimes."

"She was so bipolar man. One day she was one of the nicest people to be around. The next day, she was upset about nothing to the point she was losing her marbles," he pursed his lips and looked away from me.

"She was always that way. There was no middle ground with her. It was the best day of her life or the absolutely worst. After all this time has passed, I want to forgive her. I want to understand all these overwrought feelings of disgust—but for some selfish reason I'm struggling. Back then, I was too fascinated with her to see past the mess," I replied.

"It's not your fault, really. I think anyone in your shoes would feel those things. Girls like her, who can be so sociable and hilarious, it's easy to be fascinated by them," Stone smiled.

"But why? I understand the obvious— they were fascinated with her charm and her figure, I know— but the world didn't have to put up with her meltdowns. The world saw a beautiful exterior. I hate to be so cut and dry about it, but that's what they saw. She ended up being less fascinating and more challenging the longer we were together," I replied empathetically.

"It's easy to see all that stuff much more clearly now. Misguided

18

people show their truest qualities when their back is up against the wall and they're hurting. She was a hurting person, obviously. Hurting people tend to hurt other people. It's not your fault that it didn't work out. It was probably for the best any way..." his voice trailed off paper-thin as if he realized the parallels between what he was saying to me and his own past relationship.

When you're a young man, relationships are rarely about falling in *love,* it is not the way our shameful souls speak. The focus tended to be inexplicably more important to land a girl so sexually attractive to call your own. I had been close innumerable times prior, but no cigar, and went on my way searching for another. I knew I was a better confidant anyway, a better friend, a man converse of many of those that existed around me, so it was inevitable that many nights I could be found knee deep in books or writing alone, figuring out ways to best serve those who needed a listening ear. The world had been bestowed a wandering eye, Alec Stone readily included, and Turner Jacobs got blessed with a wandering ear. I wasn't altogether unhappy with that fact, though. My life certainly wasn't void of pleasure.

Not long after, college hit me smack in the face. I was no longer limited by or worried about my peers' opinions. I began to care about only who I wanted to be and how I was going to be it. My confidence soared skyward and like a lighthouse beaconing in the night, it triggered a larger mass of females than I knew how to handle properly. I was the same person I always had been, but with each swallow in my throat, the fears were exhausted from my flesh and body. It was naturally at that time that women flocked into my life at a lunatics pace, and stupidly, I tied myself to the wrong anchor and sank to the bottom of the ocean. A rookie mistake, but a mistake, all the same.

Jez and my affair began over night—an affair so drenched in undertones it was all but certain it would fail—and eventually became an almost three-year relationship that existed forever and ended abruptly. The fear of loneliness eventually took her and I over; really, it overtook me rather early on, and it kept two people together who had no eternal business being together. And so the prophecy fulfilled itself: all that once grows must also wither and die. Alec and I had lived the same choreographed steps for too long with different lovers. We never knew how badly we were paying for it, until our feelings rattled away in the wind like rustling leaves in the full fall night. Things are supposed to end quickly, but if they were never destined to begin, why did they? How were you supposed to end those relationships? When you're not in love any longer, it's foolish not to flee the ship. It'll drown with or without you, after all. Flee the damn ship. For me, it begged the question: What is true love in America, anyway? Some convoluted, twisted mind game that plays its hand by *not* playing its hand, doesn't speak truth, and fulfills it's own selfish desires? Something that allows fear to dictate its decision-making? Young Turner, undeniably naïve and hopeful.

Alec cracked open another beer while in the passenger seat, which again made my insides squeamish, and sank deep into thought. He spoke caustically, almost as if he were in existing in an alternate universe.

"I'm telling you all the good ones are gone," pain dripped from his voice, and I was overcome with his sullen demeanor. His gaze transfixed on the molehill-sized mountains that we passed briskly; he spoke slowly and exaggerated his pronunciations.

"Callie is marrying him. Kip, that is. I can't believe they're actually getting married. They're only 22 years old and they're getting married. I am way too young to feel like my life is over. Do you think she could really spend the rest of her life with that curly haired fruit loop of a man? I don't want to marry her so I have no right to be this angry. Still, it's like the permanent death of our relationship is finally punching me in the face. My purpose seems to get lost somewhere," he said, shaking his head.

"Purpose? Your only purpose is to be you. Your purpose or your destiny has never been tied to another human being. You're not being pathetic; you're being authentic. Do you think they're really in love, anyway? When someone cheats, they never end up with the person they cheated with," I said cautiously. It's impossibly hard to offer genuine encouragement when you are in full agreement with someone else's struggle.

"You think so? I don't know. I can't say that I know for a fact, but I like to think they aren't profoundly in love. Call me bitter, I try not to be, you know, but maybe one day when I act like the grown man I know I should be, I can wish them well," honesty burned from the fire of his tongue.

"But, and this is as enormous a but as there is, until that day comes and greets me at the front door steps, fuck them," he laughed but more madly, than humorously.

"I suppose they've come to terms with the harsh horrors and realities of a life alone, Stone. Nobody wants to be alone, you or I included. It may not be about the *love* they garner from one another, but rather, the fact they don't have to live this life in solitary confinement," I exclaimed.

"It's not for dreamers, like us. But for some, it's as good as it gets."

"Maybe, you're right, man. Maybe," he said halfheartedly.

"I don't suppose you received an invitation to the wedding?" I quipped and Stone laughed bellowing and boisterous. Even a moronic comment on my part was worth seeing my dear friend exert genuine laughter.

"Not quite. You know she's still good friends with Dave Hector, though. So he got an invitation and shared all the details with me, which was damn delightful."

22

"We should go. It would be charitable of us. We could politely double the amount of friends she has in attendance," I laughed.

"Would you go if you had been invited?" I asked, half joking.

"No freaking way. Why in the hell would I want to do that?" Stone grimaced, emphasizing the 'o' is no.

"I don't know! In a twisted way, it's your last chance to feel like you have a say in it all," I replied.

"I don't think I could handle. Imagine being in my shoes, would you do the same if Jez was getting married? I presume Dave told you the wedding was in Florida, right? Did he tell you to ask me about going to the wedding?" He asked inquisitively.

"Seriously? Are you fucking kidding me, Stone? The wedding is in Florida and you keep telling me to drive as far south as possible? I am just thinking out loud here, but last time I checked, Florida was the southern most state!" I exclaimed.

"What? I didn't know I had a master geographer on my hand. Obviously, Florida is the southern most state, but that's just a funny coincidence, Turner. You suggested Florida any way, remember? I said why not? I need some sunshine, some coastal air, you remember right?" Stone maintained.

Though I didn't believe his aloof response for a moment, we had nothing to lose by going to Florida. On second though, at least I had nothing to lose.

"It's coincidence, alright. All the more reason we should go to her wedding. And yes, I would go to Jez's wedding, if she ever decided to settle her wild ass down. I think that you and I, as Callie and Jez's longest previous relationships, owe it to ourselves to be in attendance," I stated emphatically. We both sighed in unison so beautifully there was no need to address it.

Alec's pain stemming from Callie falling in love with Kip radiated the coastline, and washed upon my shore and as his closest confidant; I could not help but take on his burden. The devil's ally had bested us both—a women that possessed too much beauty and who was all too aware of that fact already. Men are horrendously, embarrassingly weak for women. They always put the sword in the hands of beautiful woman, pacifistically asking not to be killed after they have already relinquished full control.

And as night faded on the road, all the loneliness one could muster in their nighttime brain crept into our identities, skewing them insurmountably. Solitude isn't half bad if everyone you know is living it all around you, right? Unequivocally frustrating, but sometimes Stone and I were together in our aloneness. But that would soon change. And it would change in the most unlikely of packages and timings.

Across Cobbled Alleys

Chapter 3

Unlike so many of the other people I had encountered in my life who seemed to sit dormant and dawdling, Stone possessed a keen spirit of adventure that drew people close to him. His spirit was one of Zeus; he could blend in with the overtly Christian crowd we grew up surrounded by, though less and less by the day, but also was likable and non judgmental, and could assimilate into all other varieties of human dream beings. Much of the credit for his expansive personality was due to his mother, Jan. Jan was born with the heart of ten servants combined. She embodied a deep paradox—a coexistence of wild, free and comfortable; she was a gentle adventurer. A little less full of zest than her son, her eyes contained stories untold, dripping with the condensation of life well lived. When I looked at her, I saw a future that I desired. No experiences were left unlived, no boxes left unopened, no rocks left unturned. Much like his Mother, Stone kept a watchful eye to the sky, toward God. He was rarely cautious when it came to his intense optimism for new love, new opportunities, and the virtue of life. Things changed after his girlfriend Callie cheated on him and slept with her then best friend, Kip. Alec Stone lost his moxie in one fell swoop, feeling more disappointment and disdain for the world around him. He became increasingly despondent with

Rochester. All of the sudden, because of one heartbreaking situation, his life was put on a proverbial pause where he shelved all of the optimism he once had and lost touch with the outside world. It happened so quickly.

"I cannot regress nor progress, Turner, do you see? And as such, I'm in this enormous fucking rut. There's no positive movement for me to make here... I'm just sinking in the sand and stuck."

His rut, both literal and metaphorical, grew quickly to a valley. The valley spread and grew, fluttering like a butterfly out of the cocoon for the first time. Crack by crack his hole grew wildly, as it became the Grand Canyon. He would always tell me when I was down that it didn't have to be that way, that things were only as bad as I decided they were in my heart. I never believed him when he said it, and he didn't believe me when I tried to convince him of the same.

If we allow them to, our problems can grow larger and larger, looming ominously ahead of us until they eventually break our emotional levee. I tried to assure, encourage and ease his devastating burden of a life alone, unemployed and habitually confused. But I was living the mirror image. Burdens are so relative though, aren't they? It's so much an independent decision that allows the pause of our sorrows to grow to become a canyon size rut. My own life as a testimony, most battles are fought deep within. As much as we try to pass the pain from one blue-eyed doll faced woman to the next, another human isn't capable of saving someone so lost. Stone had acquired this mentality, the mentality that told him he needed to escape from all the factors holding him back, after trying to pass his broken heart off on other girls he found amusing. Because he wasn't ready to move on, the attempts were futile and marred with issues. He couldn't connect the right way with them, for one reason or another and so he would ask himself: "Why stay where you cannot grow? Why plant where fruit cannot possibly blossom and flourish?"

The journey wasn't as haphazard as it outwardly appeared. I could see all the things that got Alec here. And such began our time *really* on the road. No more valleys that crept up slowly on the precipice. It was time to go, and go like hell. Uncle Jack Kerouac said, "Don't look back and don't be sorry," and we wouldn't leave any reason to do either.

***

After several hours on the road, a suggestion was born out of exhaustion. Desi suggested we stay with her college roommate, Sage. Sage lived about 500 miles from Rochester, in Nashville, Tennessee. Sage and Desi combined were twice as much fun and twice as much trouble as a common street gang. "Nashvegas would be really awesome place to stop. I miss those girls down there so much," Desi smiled boisterously. "Let's stop and stay with Sage and see what she's up to. She's not the type who needs a formal announcement of arrival or anything. She'll be so pumped just to have visitors at her new apartment," Desi said.

"Are you sure she won't mind two random guys staying at her place?" Stone asked.

"Nah, she's very chill. She won't have any problem with it. She's a more the merrier type of person," Desi replied.

We eased our flesh and bones into the cascading green hills of Nashville to stay with Desi's former roommate, Sage, and Sage's current roommate, Savannah.

The two girls, who Desi described as wild flower hippies, free spirited and open minded, resided not far from downtown, four miles away on the cusp of the suburbs. We pulled in late in the evening and Alec and I disappeared into an inexpensive apartment living room, while the girls reminisced in the entryway. A small dog, appearing from the kitchen, served as our companion for the evening. Stone, upon seeing the fluff ball of a puppy, jumped onto the floor and started scratching its belly. He glanced up from rubbing the belly of the pup and I could see for a moment he felt no rut; even in this small movement, he looked temporarily removed from struggle. A glimmer of progress appeared to be shining through his hazel eyes.

"Turner, this isn't so bad. Pillow for my head and couch for my body, we can have ourselves a grand adventure five hundred miles from home in good ole Nashville." To Alec, it was always an essential adventure or all gone to hell. There was no middle ground whatsoever. I chuckled, and made a cup of decaf to sip as I made up the couch to sleep on.

The first night bled away quickly as we both fell soundly asleep, even amidst the girls chatter. The next evening I began to examine Desi's former roommate more thoroughly. She was vivacious. When she talked her eyes danced madly as if they were telling the world's greatest story. Sage was a fiery Hawaiian, standing five feet small, and she kept me entertained the whole evening long. My attraction to her was nearly instant—but not at all physical. Her witty banter, fast darting glances and room-enveloping laugh stole the spotlight. Behind the witticisms and heavily pronounced laughter, I noticed what seemed to be pain. Sweet, deep rooted anger well below her surface, sorrow and frustration.

"Life at this age, it's about having a damn good time. I love to go out, dance, drink, and laugh a lot. That's what breaks the monotony of having to work every day and put up with the bull shit of all of these other people, you know?" She routinely joked about her constant need to be drunk. She was draped in a mysterious personal history that I ached to figure out. Conversely, she drank more slowly than anyone I'd ever seen— perhaps, as if to savor each and every last drop of the poison.

Alec, Desi, Sage and I headed south into the Nashville city

center to find a bar. We parked in a ramp with sparse, grim reaper like lighting and walked through a petrifying alleyway to McBlag's Irish Pub. It was dank and rank but cozy and empty; after all it was a Monday night. Only the most dedicated of bar rats show on Monday nights. Never one to frequent bars prior to that year—22—the most God-awful and surreal of my life, I bought the first round and sat next to Sage.

"Why do you look so sad?" Sage asked, catching me off guard.

"Me? I'm not sad. I'm exhausted," I replied, a bit surprised by her direct question.

"No, it's not that. You look sad. I've heard a lot about you from my Desi. I know you are a happy go lucky go-getter kind of guy, not the type to easily give up. Tonight, when I met you, you looked a little bit like you've given up," she spoke forwardly. Trying not to be hurt by her words, I glanced all around at the neon lights of the bar.

"I'm just a little bit lost, I guess. I've never really been lost. All the sudden I feel like there is a ceiling on my life, like I am limited in what I can really do or accomplish," I replied earnestly.

"I understand that. Life can be a bitch. You seem like the kind of person who will get what they want. Maybe you need to be more patient. I know I sure as hell do. My mom always said to us as kids, one of the most important things we can do is be persistent," she said caught somewhere between philosophical and drunkenness.

"You will figure it out too, Sage," I said back.

"What do you mean? How do you know what I'm feeling?" Sage said.

"Your eyes, when I look into them, they tell me everything. They are the windows to the soul, you know," I darted back, catching her off guard.

"Confess your sins and your sorrows. I can handle them," I said. I often said things like this to get people to open up.

"Maybe later. I don't even know you yet."

"We should change that," I flirted.

"Could we? I'm interested in getting to know you better," she flirted back, her devilish grin displayed.

Sage danced gracefully and asked me to dance with her. For some reason, despite my complete lack of dancing ability, I agreed and danced we did. Floating across the glossy floor, my heel began bleeding from trying to keep up with her impeccable dancing ability. She led me step by step. I complimented her and she played it off confidently, and the song ended but we did not.

Three hours later, we were tangled, entwined in her sheets. She told me she wanted to talk (which we'd been doing all night) but eager to hear more of her story, I happily obliged listening intently. Her brown boat eyes swam slowly across my shore rising tide to my north. Her lips opened quietly, each breath she drew was somber and all that was left was she and I and the words clanking the walls. Holding me like she would

32

never let go, I knew morning would soon be upon us. Birds chirped loudly outside the first floor apartment window mimicking the morning and wind blew branches into the exterior walls. Her brow furrowed heavily, her eyes fluttered as to dismiss droplets of atom size tears.

"Turner, what's it all about? Why do guys always leave me? I always do what I am supposed to do. I guess I don't get what it is that I'm missing."

She paused for a moment heavily.

"Honestly, it makes me feel plain. Sometimes I feel small, not small as in my midget stature, but like a small human being—someone who doesn't stand out in a crowd," she sighed.

"I wasn't made just to be somebody's wife, you know. I have so many dreams I want to accomplish," she said as to assure me.

I interjected like I always did at this age, with a zest beyond my experiences: "You know, it's really not about him or you. Sometimes it's the simple fact that the "us" didn't work and the two of you were meant for greener pastures. Sure, it may feel like you've been hit in the head, repeatedly with a baseball bat, but love, it will eventually get better. And you seriously think you don't stand out? You're out of this world; do you know that? You're your own planet in your own solar system. You're engaging and deep and curious and full of life. Don't for any person, any human being, change any of that," I spoke to her with feelings I resurrected from the pit of my stomach.

"Love will find you. It'll track you down when you least expect it," I charmed.

She smiled softly and chuckled just enough to show me she had received my message, even if she didn't believe it. "My ex was eleven years older than me too, which probably didn't help the situation either. We were sort of experiencing different phases of life. I was in college and he was 30 but desperately wishing he was in college," she lamented cackling her hocus pocus laugh.

"I mean, if a guy can't commit at age 30, he's probably full of commitment issues," I assured her.

"Right? My mom said the same thing over and over again. You're sweet, Turner. Almost too much that way; like you've not been hurt before," she said.

Rolling out of our spider web, swiftly sleep stole her from my company. Pressing bitter cold lips to her cheek, I slurred "goodnight dear," and we rejoined flesh on flesh chasing sleep, two hurting people trying to understand that hurt in a mortal manner. There was nothing sexual, physical, or selfish about it; it was simple soul searching peregrination. It was a moment that turned both of our lives on their heels.

***

I awoke hazy to my sister bellowing for us to get out of

bed. Like every day before it, I wanted nothing less than to leave the warmth of sticky springtime sheets. For the past ten hours, I'd been genuinely distracted, regardless of how minuscule those ten hours might have been in the presence of all the hours we live, I was pleased and complete.

Stone entered Sage's bedroom reading the emotion on my face. Bashful, his best played emotion; his face fell into a cheeky grin. As we began packing the car to re-embark on our journey, his silence broke.

"You dog! What happened? You booted me to the couch, so I deserve a detailed account of your endeavors!" Stone gleaned with eager anticipation.

"Nothing really happened man, but still, it was freaking magical. I actually felt connected to another human being, albeit momentarily."

"What? That's all I get after I sacrificed the bed for a lousy couch? Damn it to hell Jacobs! I need more. Come on! Give me more!" Looking longingly across the parking lot, the rain began to sprinkle on our rested, rejuvenated heads.

"I just want to save her, Stone. She has this untapped potential that she doesn't even recognize on her insides. Her heart is gold and her eyes are like lampshades to her soul. I want to throw her in the car with me and take her to a far away dream land where our pasts do not exist and we do not miss anything or anyone." Alec was direct in his response, for it was morning and he wasn't joking yet.

"Valiant, Turner. It really is. You always get yourself in these situations. But you know she'll never be truly saved by a guy like you. She'll wander aimlessly, searching with great hope but never really being satisfied. A man cannot simply save a woman. A woman has to save herself. And from what I can tell, she's a strong woman. She'll save herself just fine when the timing is right," he quipped.

"I sure hope so. She's the most captivating human being I've met in far too long. I hope there's something more than wandering aimlessly. Some people need other people to do the saving, but maybe you're right. Maybe she's the kind who's strong enough she'll end up saving herself," I responded.

"Hell, I don't always have the answer, but I do know you won't be the one to save Sage. She'll look in all the places where guys like us do not exist. Women do all they can not to be saved," he professed as he ran back into the apartment to collect the rest of his things.

I walked back inside to take a quick shower but I waited for Sage to finish first. I sat down with Stone, who ate cereal at a barstool at the faux granite countertop in the kitchen. Savannah and Desi sat on the covered porch talking, and Savannah smoked a joint while the rain dripped over the edge of the awning. It was a soft, pensive springtime morning.

Sitting there with Stone, his words were strong as

whiskey to my paper heart. I always erred on the side of being hopeful in the past—and I wanted to remain hopeful that any person could be saved with the right medicine. But by now, I was jaded and seasoned enough to know this was not always the case. I prayed it would be different for the beautiful Sage Pree.

Across Cobbled Alleys

Chapter 4

Dripping with water after exiting a shower that was easily older than I was, and nearly completely filled with rust, I left feeling dirtier after ten minutes under the single stream nozzle. "Guys, it's about time we hit the road. James Ryan is anticipating us in less than three hours."

"What? You told me we're heading there today?" Stone asked.

"Well, yeah we're only three hours away or so. Remember you said the other night that you wanted a place to stay and we can stay with him for free," Desi beamed.

"That's true, I just didn't realize we were heading straight there. But I have nowhere better to be at," Stone replied laughing.

My sister paced anxiously, but with grace that told me she could just as well be an angel. Blonde hair in a loose-bouncy set of curls, blue eyes glowing, she had on a turquoise sundress. With a cup of coffee and olive shoulder bag in tow, my sister was crammed into the backseat of the car with our pillows and blankets.

"It's finally time to see my man! Hurry on up, boys!" she proclaimed loudly, referring to her then-boyfriend James Ryan. We said our goodbyes to Sage and company.

"Know what you're worth, sweet little Tennessee peach," I addressed her by the nickname I had made for her during our drunken stupor.

She pulled me under an oak tree near the apartment building, and drew me in close.

"You made my life last night. Thanks for everything. Seriously, every thing you said, I won't ever forget it," she said.

"I won't forget it either. You're impossible to forget. I hope one day our paths cross again. Don't be a stranger," I said.

We shared a long hug; I kissed her forehead and then departed the cloudy, gray skies of Nashville. Somber sober goodbyes always lead to a melancholic stomach turning restlessness because no one else understands the gravity of it all at that moment except you.

I had never met James Ryan before. Desi talked about him ad-nauseam though, so I felt like I knew him quite well. He was prim and proper with a deliberate crease in his hair combed to the side, and sported a collared long sleeve shirt even when he would lounge around the house. He was well spoken, well liked and by all estimations, well intentioned. I could not say that about most of the guys my sister had dated. He lived in Birmingham, Alabama where he attended medical school. He was highly motivated to succeed—from all she told me, I was sure he would. Something remained missing from his outwardly flawless life, Desi said. An emptiness existed that couldn't be explained and no matter how many books he read or scholars he conversed with, sometimes he transparently showed an emptiness that could not be explained. Perhaps my delightful, caring sister in his life would fill the emotional void. Her vivacious zeal for life could be contagious to anyone around her. She breathed humble air and made fun appear out of thin air. And she believed uncommonly devoutly in love. Desi believed in love like almost no other person breathing life in this celestial galaxy. She had a deep seeded idealism that told her love was real and it existed everywhere, in various forms. The matter of fact was that she thought James Ryan might be her one and only, even if they weren't even technically boyfriend and girlfriend. No one wants to live a cynical life, but the "one and only" ideology always seemed terribly far-fetched to me. I hoped for her soft spirits sake she would prove my doubts to be misguided.

***

The road after Nashville, while not completely foreign, was not well known by any of the three of us. It was a long straight shot south to Birmingham. The day moved slowly as the brooding springtime song of a Sunday sinner in the sweet South. Clouds blanketed the day, painting our emotions with a brushstroke of melancholy. The instrument laden music of angel-voiced Icelandic singer Jonsi played loudly as our tires spiraled end over end on the water filled highway. After two times through the album, Stone broke what had become an eerie silence.

"Do you think I'll find love again, man? I am what I am, sure, fallen and sinful but I know I have a lot to offer. It's annoying that no one else can seem to see that anymore."

My eyes traced the wood dash in the car. Feeling similarly, I told Stone all that I knew to say.

"In due time old friend, in due time."

He stared off into the rolling Alabama countryside, mesmerized, unsure and obviously less than appeased with my token response. Our friendship was anything but a token one.

I continued, "You know, life is so cyclical. Some woebegone gal can stroll in and out of your life in just two blinks and perhaps, it'll take four times that many blinks for another to appear. But by gosh, one will eventually appear," I tried desperately to believe myself. Did I truly believe each person had another person waiting for them? We both needed to learn the greatest of all virtues—patience.

"I don't know if it will take us until our deaths but I hope one day I'm patient enough to sit still and wait for God to work in my life," he said.

I marinated on his response and gave him a friendly half-smile and placed my water bottle to my lips.

"Patience, though, is a son of bitch," grimacing and shaking his head. "But I'm ready man. I swear it. It's time for me to find that love-thing again, if it really exists."

Funny, people all around pondered the same thing each

day since the dawn of time.

Hours passed, rain pushed away to the west and we arrived in downtown Birmingham. Alec found the pool patio to pacify our time while Desi and James Ryan reconnected.
Stone and I napped while my sister had a dinner date at a sushi place with James Ryan. It was the first time on our travels that I stopped to breath the limitless air deeply. It was the first moment I began to truly relax. I thought about sitting on a beach laden with women adorned in bikinis. It was a simple and cathartic thought. Sometimes the tired eyed traveler, even the greatest warrior of the road, needs the fresh spring air on his face and a childlike dream of happy things in his head.

Alec and I wandered into the downtown section of Birmingham later that night. It was the last day in May and heat rose from the scorching pavement. The night offered some peace, cooling to a more manageable 75 degrees. Our Alabama adventure was but a mere pit stop; a rest station on the spirited road of life where self-discovery can occur in the shortest segment of time in the most off the beaten path places. But that's all it was, we knew as much, and Alec and I began conjuring up our next destination.

"You see that girl over there, the one in the turquoise bikini?" Alec whispered.

"She'd be hard to miss," I replied.

"She reminds me of this girl I know from Georgia. She's our old

42

buddy Dave Hector's cousin, Blythe. She's a goddess," he said, smiling Grinch like.

"I met her once when we were younger. She seemed like a nice girl," I replied.

Exasperated, Stone laughed.

"Nice girl? A nice girl? She would be nicer if she were spending her nights with me on a beach somewhere with drinks in our hands. I wonder what she's up to now anyway," he laughed.

"You could call her. It might be a bit formal. We both know you stalk her on Facebook, so you already know what she's up to," I said laughing loudly at my burn.

He smirked at me, but I saw the light bulb go off in Alec's head and he pulled out his dated cell phone and punched the keys. The phone was so antiquated; it was essentially a brick that just so happened to make phone calls sometimes, too.

"Blythe my dear! Hello," He spoke loudly, chuckling after her emphatic greeting back. A slow as molasses Southern drawl, which conveyed relaxation and evoked pictures of simpler times, buzzed through the telephone wires. This was the pace of the South; slow and steady. They chatted for a few moments, and thereafter, Stone scribbled an address in electric blue ink on a crumbled up yellow post it note he pulled from his pocket.

"242 Forest Park Drive, Alpharetta, Georgia, my friend," Alec stated.

"Please tell me that is her address, Alec? Please tell me she wants us to come over to the ATL?" I joked with semi-serious undertones.

"You're damn right it is! You are going to be pleasantly surprised my friend. This girl—she's as good a southern belle as you're going to find. She's not exactly your cup of tea, she's a brunette after all, but I hope to enjoy her quite a bit. She said she has friends, too. And not to mention, she said we could stay at her place for a night or two while her parents are out of town. We just keeping winning, Turner! I told you this whole thing was meant to be," he said, elated.

Ever disinterested in the matters of money, and always finding new ways to honor the cheap Dutchman within, Stone continued this trend until forever. I loved it and loathed it equally, but this was one of the nights I absolutely loved it indeed. With little money in our possession, and what money we did have pretty well allocated to our future road wanderings, there was no better solution than a free place to stay. Too, it was a better solution than sleeping in a bank parking lot in some backwoods location like many wayward messengers of the road had done before us.

"Sounds like a winning situation to me. I guess it's to Georgia we go, Stone," I cooed. And I couldn't help but sing Georgia, Georgia repeatedly and Ray Charles would have been proud.

At once, Desi returned to the car where we were now waiting. She had make up streaks of navy and black down her

44

cheeks.

"Des—what's wrong?" I struggled.

"We're not staying here. God, he's such an asshole. Just another asshole. He— just— he said it's over for good this time," she sobbed and I grabbed her into my arms and wrapped her up, hiding her face from the people around us.

"Let's get you out of here. You don't need to be around this," Stone interjected.

"Brother? She looked up, tears still running, I want to keep going with you guys. I know I said I might stay here, then go back home, but obviously that's not happening," she whimpered.

"Desi, you know I would love that, but you know really should go back home, you have school and everything," I despised my innate logical side in that moment.

"Not anymore I don't."

"You can't just drop out, you've been doing so well—"
Desi cut me off abruptly.

"I dropped out last year. I just didn't want to bother you and parents with all that. They can be so hard on me, you know."

"Really? Seriously?" I muttered.

"Yup. That school thing just doesn't for me. I'm ready to go. Where are we going, Alec?" she said turning her attention to Stone.

"You can't just drop a bomb on me like that and not elaborate on it at all? Why'd you drop out? When?" I was perplexed.

"Not now. I don't feel like talking about it. I've had an awful night. If we talk about it, I'll just feel worse," she exclaimed.

"Okay, fine Des," I managed to mutter, knowing that I would only inflame her anger and sadness if I pressed her for more information.

"Woop Woop! We are Georgia bound! And trust me, there are plenty of men out there who cannot wait to know you," he smiled ear to ear.

An adventure is made all the more merry when those you love join in on it. Sometimes on paper it doesn't make sense to continue, but who decided what the rules were in the chess game that is life? We need not comply with someone else's version of the truth. So we continued on for Georgia, creating and finding our own version of it.

***

We drove as the night howled on madly. The twists and turns, not far from the city of Atlanta, maintained an ambiance of the rural country that sent ominous vibrations through my spine. Atlanta has a unique greenness to it that most people do not expect. It's unmistakably colorful and flowing, and it's city limits sprawl far beyond the general metropolitan area of the city.

We pushed on toward Blythe's house, despite exhaustion

rounding our eyes in the form of deep, dark circles, and pulled up to a two-story brick home that was well kept near a myriad of homes that looked the same. It had an L-shaped drive with a dated silver Mercedes Benz in the garage and a newer model Chevy Tahoe next to it. Soccer moms in cities all over the country seemed to need Tahoe's and Escalades and Denali's to take their brigade from one practice or commitment to the next. Chasing some American dream, dream, dream—not really sure what that dream was or the purpose of it in the first place, but pushing, pulling and propelling their last bit of will to attain it. Please, God, in the blue heaven skies, let my future play out differently than this, I thought to myself. I don't want an overpriced home in a squatty suburban neighborhood with "good schools," BBQs and soccer practice. I want to exist in happiness, free of condemnation, with like age peers on my own terms that share similar ideas.

Before we could exit the car, Desi, who was out cold the past few hours, awoke to the shrieks of excitement only miserable average girls offer. Alec was of course the main course for the average girls. I was satisfied being relegated to the appetizer for her friends. Blythe greeted him by jumping into his arms unabashedly, and he released one of his forced laughs where his eyes crease shut nearly completely and his dimples begin to show. He was uncomfortable enough to crawl out of his pale white skin. But no matter, like a champion, he pressed onward with his eye on the prize: rent-free sleep and a somewhat attractive girl that in no way looked like the girl we had seen at the Birmingham pool earlier that day. We entered the beautiful, but simple, middle class home. Sitting on the suede taupe sofa were two girls, approximately 20 years old. The first gal, a freckle faced redhead, was the last girl on the Earth anyone would willingly sleep with. The second, an average build, sandy haired girl with emerald green timid eyes looked like Marilyn Monroe next to her carrot topped friend. I wanted little to do with either. Just a warm bed and maybe a late night supper would satisfy my soul. Hell, to avoid the potentially disastrous situation playing out in front of my face, I would even avoid the dinner.

Alec continued to be doted on by Blythe as we waltzed around the house. The two friends, later identified as "Alyssa" and "Amie," were in tow. I played it coy, much unlike my typical self, hoping to turn them off my trail. Forgetting all I know about women, the more brazen and coy I became, the more I was fawned over. My exhaustion was inhibiting even my best passes at resistance. They both announced that they were single to the entire group within minutes of our arrival. This fact only scared my fatigued soul further.

What in the world is wrong with these women? Daddy issues are running rampant in America today; society has warped the view of almost all young girls as to what a *healthy*

48

relationship should look like. People stay with the wrong people for too long because they're too scared or too lonely to find an escape route. Years stack up, and too many people begin to lose their hope, merely settling in with whomever they are with and getting married in hope of mending their discord. Though it appears that some people find this approach logical, which is mind numbing to me, it's ultimately the worst humanly possible decision they could make. It causes them to fall into a dismal despair that cannot be repaired with all the self-help books in the world. It made me painstakingly sad. And angry, too, that the faces of wide-eyed young lovers didn't know *love* at all. The way Alyssa and Amie threw themselves at me, it was apparent they were clueless about love. Then again, who was I to be critical? I was equally illiterate.

Blythe led us to our quarters for the night. The room, two full beds with green comforters, reminded me of a place I'd stayed in the mountains years before. All of the furniture was maple glazed and there was animal artwork strewn across the room. We placed our things on the cold wood floor and I decided to sprawl across the bed nearest the window. Not ten minutes later, a voice emerged from the echoing silence.

"Alec, are you still hungry? It's not a problem for me to make something... it'll only take a few minutes," I smiled to myself, knowing she wanted nothing more than to feed him a Blythe sandwich.

Alec, for either his interest in her or free food, I wasn't all too sure, willingly complied and followed Blythe down stairs shuffling feet quickly.

An hour passed and I wrestled with the sheets. Sleepless, as always, I took the stairway slowly as each step creaked loudly. The two others girls and Desi had disappeared hours earlier, heading to bed in the basement after I left them feeling relatively bored with life. A moaning and groaning of sorts could be heard coming from the next room, and my ears were shocked into frozen silence. Peering eyelash over eyelash around into the living room, I saw a butt naked Blythe on top of the ole bastard, Alec Stone. Her small breasts were triangular and flopped in a bouncy ball fashion to and fro. Alec had a thing for girls with "sporty b-cups," and Blythe fit this particular mold with near perfection. She shrieked at him to keep going repeatedly and from what I could tell, he obliged her request.

"Faster, Alec. More. I want more of you," she moaned.

"You get it all, baby. I'll give you more," he replied fervently.

"I've wanted this for so long, you have no idea," she mumbled, moaning.

"God, me too. Your body feels fucking incredible," Stone remarked.

Not being a fan of homemade living room pornography, I decided it was time to quickly sneak into the kitchen for a sandwich. I opened the stainless steel Frigidaire and pulled out a wrap and three slices of turkey lunchmeat. I washed the head of lettuce and accessorized my sandwich further with mayo and mustard before rushing up the stairs. I sat at the desk and opened up a notebook. Journeys had always led me into enlightenment. Pressing the pen to the page, I scribbled on a tattered piece of yellow paper: "Seek wholeheartedly and you will find."

Oddly, even though I had just left home and was still so young in the spectrum of the Earthy flesh, I felt more awakened than before. It became apparent in my head I'd likely never come home to live through the mundane Michigan madness again. A chill raised every hair on my skin and I devoured the sandwich knowing my only hope was in what might lie ahead. Because it doesn't matter where you go, just that you go.

Across Cobbled Alleys

Chapter 5

Burnt bacon and pancake batter brought me from the dead to the living the following morning. Picking up my gym shorts that found their way to the floor during the night, I moseyed to the dining area. There sat Stone and all of the girls except Desi, who was sleeping in per usual. Stone shot me a glance and tipped his head toward the sliding porch door. His eyes were anxious and panic stricken.

"Jacobs, look, before you judge me"... his words shot like minuscule bullets from his chapped lips. I allowed for the gravity of his horribly awkward situation to sink in. He stammered and stuttered, a behavior only normal when he was entirely shaken. "Well, I had sex with Blythe last night," he grimaced.

I stood emotionless like a statue, acting as if this were unremarkable information.

"She is kind of hot, right? She has really sexy eyes and sporty B's. You know that I love both of those things," he croaked.

I remained silent and stoic.

"Jacobs, say something! She's not a bad girl—other than the exception she thinks last night means we're a couple or something. That could be complicated going forward."

All the silence spilled over and I cried out, buckling on the patio floor, laughing so deeply tears were running down my

52

cheeks.

"You and Blythe. You slept with Blythe. This is fantastic. I can't wait until ole Dave finds out."

Dave was our 23-year-old friend Dave Hector. Dave was a childhood classmate of ours, who was slightly overweight in the midsection, but not in the rest of his body, with a hairline chasing the ceiling and apathy toward most everything in life. He was kind hearted and full of satirical humor when he was at his best; however, crippling anxiety often inhibited his ability to get out and spend time with people.

The real dichotomy Stone faced, beyond having sex with a girl he barely knew, was that Blythe was Dave's favorite cousin. In fact, we always suspected Dave had an unusual crush of sorts on Blythe. For obvious reasons, the less that Dave knew about Alec Stone seducing his beloved cousin, the better. Stone and I decided it was best to let sleeping dogs lie and hope that Dave never found out the truth of the matter.

Stone stewed back and forth on the patio anxiously until Blythe appeared in a yellow oversized tee shirt and short-shorts, the former of which belonged to Alec. "Breakfast is served, boys. Good morning Alec!" She gushed, while she staring solely at Alec. "Ah yeah, hey, good morning," he replied to her.
She kissed his cheek and his face became flushed.
"I figured y'all would be hungry after last night, so I made so much food," she giggled. Quickly catching herself, she continued

sending a glance my way, "tired from the traveling and all, of course." She was clearly smitten with him and had no regrets about the evening. Stone reeked of adulation, and Blythe showed no signs of letting up. It wasn't the first time I'd felt invisible like that. It certainly wouldn't be the last either.

"You bet we are. That was sweet of you to think of us, Blythe," I interjected.

"My pleasure of course. Y'all my guests, after all," she spoke sunnily.

We sat around a brushed oak table, with dings and dents on most of the edges. Much to my chagrin, Alyssa and Amie were present. They were still not accounted for. Per my ever-good luck, the redheaded friend, Alyssa, was growing quite fond of me. She sloshed food into her gullet haphazardly—flecks of which fell around her plate, on the floor, and near my feet. Her demeanor was altogether friendly, but I didn't give her a chance. I was much too young and much too stupid to look for things beyond the surface of her skin. Especially after the heartbreak of my not so distant past, anything relational seemed purposeless. I was too jaded and sour to look beyond what I could physically see.

Meanwhile, Amie was twisting her sandy colored hair around a slender index finger and growing far more disinterested in blessing us with her presence. It was one crazy congregation of people. From the outside world, the semblance

54

of human lives that intersected at 242 Forest Park drive was normal, even mundane. Yet the whole world existed beyond the reality of those people in that small room. The world seemed to pause within the confines of our conversations.

All the while, Stone was grimacing and fumbling his speech. I assumed he was getting a handy underneath the great oak table. Desi was still sound asleep, baby blanket in tow. Despite having nineteen years of wisdom at her disposal, it was essential that "Señor" her infamously torn yellow blanket be at her side nightly. Maybe she wasn't breastfed long enough. No one knew what her infatuation with it was. Not even myself, her own brother.

After likely finishing his happy ending, Alec excused himself from the table and much to my displeasure, didn't come back for nearly ten minutes leaving me alone with the girls. I've always been a talker, verbose and thorough. But this bunch was testing my last ounce of patience. When had I grown so impatient?

"There he is! Where did you disappear to big guy?" I proclaimed far too exuberantly drawing all attention from me to Stone. "Quick phone call, nothing big. Checking in at home. I know you're all excited to see me but I was only gone like ten minutes," he quipped. All the girls chuckled and Blythe smiled insanely, the way that all insane and in love girls do. I understood that look in her eyes. A look I'd possessed and that I'd seen a few times before. The look that speaks of our innate desire for someone to be somewhat insane for us, theoretically, until that insane love is on our doormat, available and waiting, in a moment we decide we'd rather be alone living a life of solitude and freedom.

Casted well into middle class American dreams, we washed up and got ready for the road that very day. Stone was the one usually expressing restlessness, but on this occasion it was me who had overstayed my welcome by twenty-four hours.

Alec was exerting his preponderance on Blythe, who was willing and pleased to allow it. He found himself knee deep in a no-good love affair, as if there was any other kind. Not that he was even aware of it at the time. He had an extraordinary ability to block things out. He could only see from his own distorted point of view.

Blythe sat legs crossed, hair pea-cocking around her oval head, and she was mesmerized completely with the boy she had started referred to as "Big Al."

Often times, I would love a girl the same blind optimism, but it wouldn't last. Cynicism would take root. But the youthful optimism Blythe displayed—I was hungry for that. How was she so outwardly pursuant of what she desired? I silently wondered why I always found myself so easily distracted by the opposite sex. I struggled to be content when I was in a relationship. How many times had I felt the way that Blythe felt? For a young man sifting through the all involved world, complexities are part of

56

the daily ritual. And in my daydream mind I realized, sometimes there are no clear answers to why we are the way we are.

As Blythe bothered Stone to join us on our road endeavors, I sat outside in the Georgia sunshine, which produced a seasoning unlike many other places, and marinated in all of its holiness. If only I'd be able to find resolve in the medium presented me. My wounds so deep—ocean size holes in my hearts arteries—I'm as much complete as I ever will be *probably*. While we spend our lives hopelessly searching for a souls distinctive counterpoint in another, the world passes us by. But sweet love, when it is found in all its glory, there is not another feeling as poignant on God's green earth.

***

The morning dew on the grass was silvery and sheen, and I threw my belongings back into the car. Desi, dressed comfortably in sweatpants, a Patagonia fleece coat and signature FSU hat, was road ready as she bounced into the front passenger seat.

"Ready to go, Stone?" I beckoned.

"Turner, hey, wait up. I'm coming," yelled the female voice from the stairs. Stone walked up to the car, his face wreaked of defeat.

"So, Blythe is coming..." and seconds later Blythe ran out with clothes, boots and a curling iron bursting out of a large maroon bag and a worn hounds tooth suitcase in tow.

"You must be the world's fastest packer, Blythe," I smiled, trying hard not to roll my eyes.

"Actually, I did it last night. I kind of thought if you were going to Florida anyway it wouldn't be a problem if I came, too. But I sure don't want to impose," she quizzically stated.

"It's no imposition at all. We don't know exactly where we'll be staying but Stone, you can share your room, right?" I smirked and rolled my eyes at Stone, who looked somewhere between perturbed and pleased. His demeanor was incalculable.

"That would be amazing! Is that alright with you, Alec?"
She was too happy for her own good. It was hard to root against her; even if it was my best friend she was complicating life for.

We filled the five-hour drive to Florida from Northern Georgia with lots of conversation, mostly instigated by Blythe.

"So, Turner how's your love life? Is there a special girl back home? There must be considering the fact you didn't try to hook up with Amie or Alyssa."

"On the contrary my dear Blythe..." I said, goofily.

"What do you mean by that?" She asked, filled with ingénue.

"I mean, the opposite of that. No ladies in my life at all right now," I replied with a forced smile hoping she wouldn't ask for more. Naturally, she did.

"Oh! You really should've gone after one of my friends. They thought you were so cool!"

58

"I guess I'm just not up for that," I sighed, trying to act like I meant it.

"Awe, did you go through a break up recently? I had one not too long ago. They suck don't they?" She said.

"Yeah, awhile back I went through one. They sure do suck," I retorted weakly.

"Lucky for you, you are only a few hours away from being on a beach where thousands of girls our age will be, most of them looking for a nice guy like you," she giggled. If only she knew me. I laughed to myself. I was entirely positive there were many girls caked in sunscreen on the beach in Florida looking for guys who lacked the movie star muscle, only flexed their mental muscle, and who loved to write and read. Sure, there would be a *long* list awaiting me.

After a handful of hours later, two fill ups and a break for food at a South Georgia Chick Fil A, we neared our destination and we rolled down the windows. Instantly, the perfume of salty ocean air filled our lungs. We rounded Front Beach Road and the sparkling turquoise waters along the highway had us completely entranced. Beach Side was a holiday destination for my family for many years, and I knew no better way to find peace than at the beach. Ironically, Beach Side was only a mere 30 minutes from where Callie's wedding would be happening. The coincidence became even more peculiar.

People were walking, riding bikes and running all over

Beach Side as we pulled up to our condo. It was probably the least expensive condo in all of Beach Side, where million dollar plus homes lined the shore and the streets. The houses were Mediterranean in style, featured large distinguished porches, torch style lighting and white picket fences. The condo section of the complex was also finished in a Mediterranean motif and impeccably well maintained. As we ran up the steps to our mouse grey and white condo that stood three narrow stories, I stopped and took in the sticky air. If this place wasn't heaven, birds chirping all around me even in the dead of night, the thrill of people everywhere smiling, laughing and drinking merrily—I didn't know if it could be found.

Stone couldn't sit still, and neither could I. We couldn't simply unpack and lie around. Even the several hour drive southward, couldn't settle us down.

We almost immediately began running wild toward the cobble stone paths that led to the beach. Stone oodled and awed, cat calling, yipping and burning up, at all the innumerable passing potential. The glow of a campfire illuminated the fraction of the beach we approached swiftly. How contagious Stone's enthusiasm was! His eyes were fireflies dancing around the crescent moon; a mass of hope was dripping from his words in abundance. It was almost as if Blythe wasn't in tow with us and his possibilities were absolutely, unequivocally endless. We approached the warm beachside fire, surrounded by a

60

community of people, varying in age, banging on drums in a cult-tribunal fashion as the drunks around it danced gleefully on. We passed them with cautious eyes, trying not to stare at their unashamed vibrancies. Feet covered in the stickiness of sand, we pressed onward down to the shoreline. Ahead, in the blackest of nights, a dozen or so addicts lit their bongs. As we approached the congregation of teens, all the light surrounding the group went instantly dim. Eeriness naturally followed. Not to be outdone by the tribal ceremony behind us, 100 paces ahead stood a man signaling a spaceship, arms stretched to the sky, feet in the sea, apparently trying to jump into the orange glow of the moon and attempting to be sucked back to outer space.

"God brought out the strangest group of people in the world tonight; and he brought them out just for us," Stone stated in a matter of fact manner. I nodded in full agreement.

We followed the crickets as they chirped in unison and the tree lilies fell with consistency and we found our way back to the rental home. The Florida shore exuded forgiveness of sins yet to come. For now, we needed rest. The only thing missing from our journey thus far had been adequate sleep. So, in search of rejuvenation, we walked into our chosen chambers of the condo and our minds went there separate ways, each person chasing their own nightmares and dreams.

The following day, we awoke to bluebird skies and the glimmer of sunshine. I walked out on the porch that overlooked the town center laden with palm trees and the buzz of people, sipping on warm dark roast coffee. As I stood there, I knew this was why I came along. Thinking on the porch of a condo in Beach Side was better than falling in love. The creases around my mouth displayed a larger smile than my face could contain. As I got lost in my own deliriously elated thoughts, the rest of the group eventually found me. Everyone was in agreement that we spend the day at the beach, so we packed up a cooler and our things and headed down the cobbled pathways.

The air was ripe with challenge presented by beautiful bikini clad women and the entire group looked hopeful. To the left, waltzed a blond with a red and white striped suit boasting her bodacious figure, followed by a group of faux blondes that were of similar size, stature and appeal. To the right, there was a group of Phi Mu Sorority sisters, adorned in oversized t-shirts with their sorority letters noted boldly on the front. The pickings were thick, but Stone was bogged down with the slender 110 lb. frame of Blythe.

Blythe, sporting a black bandeau bikini, napped with her freckled face down in a towel on the pearliest pasted white sands. Alec had suggested she come join us while in the middle of love making—a suggestion we'd both come to regret— and one he found little solace in. While Blythe had a few redeeming qualities, her most notable characteristic was her ability to pester Stone incessantly. I found it quite amusing, because she

62

wasn't actually annoying, but to Alec, she was like nails screeching down on a chalkboard. I began to feel bad for Blythe when the writing was on the wall that they were entering into a miserable agreement with one another. How could Alec Stone possibly attempt to rescue another person when he was altogether lost? It didn't outwardly appear to be his best move. The only possible endings were that he turned it all around or it ended in a complete crash and burn.

Frisbee flying from my hand to Stone 30 yards down wind, we jostled and jumped voraciously, life oozing with each particle of sand stuck between our toes. We'd gone coastal—and Blythe postal—when the idea of Dave Hector visiting was tossed into the cursed airwaves. None of us actually believed the ultra-conservative, less than adventurous Dave would make the cross-country journey, but life has a funny way of playing its hand sometimes.

And there Stone and I sat on the worlds most beautiful beach, all starry-eyed sprung; sleep still begging at the corner of our eyes for mercy after running the beach rampant. The Kerouac pages devoured by us both, casted a new light on our own lives. Abstract love found as the youth (and not so youthful) engaged in folly for another spring on a Floridian beach. "If we just keep to ourselves, not pursuing women, traveling all around this God blessed country and sitting dormant *really* living?" Stone objects.

I shook my head, a definitive "no" and we decided we'd do as we pleased regardless because life is not to be confined or limited; go climb each sand dune to the endless glitzing stars of the Floridian shore. Climb until you cannot any longer.

"Dave will be here soon enough. We better get the Wild West out of our systems," I said to Alec.

Alec scoffed.

"Sure, let's. Do you think will never be out of our systems altogether?"

"Only time will tell," I replied optimistically.

***

Half a week of hamburger flipping, beach hopping, restaurant venturing and paddle boarding excursions later, Dave Hector himself greeted us. He exited his red Mercedes, which was much less nice than what he perceived it to be, and strutted slowly to the porch. Proper in some respects, he rang the doorbell, but when no one answered, he entered the house.

"Turner? Alec? Blythe?" He called out whimsically.

"Up here, my good man," Stone shouted from the third level of the condo.

Dave entered the room in his khaki shorts with cargo pockets, and a brightly colored Polo shirt I had given him before his first job interview. He hugged all of us and plopped on the

64

couch.

"Thanks for having me down on such short notice. I just really needed to get away. Things at home...they've been dicey of late," he sheepishly smiled

"Have you been okay? Why have things been dicey?" Blythe interjected, spilling with matronly concern for her cousin.

"Well, uh, yeah. Things with Mom and Dad are confusing. I'm not sure they are going to get past their marital discord thing time around. And living at home was driving me nuts, so I knew I needed to clear my mind from all of their problems and the repetitive pains of living in Rochester. Not to mention, I don't feel well lately. Just sick to my stomach and stuff almost all the time," Dave shared, sadly.

Just what these repetitive things bothering Dave might be, none of us actually knew. In many ways, his life had been easy. His cars, his college, his expenses—all were funded entirely by his Grandparents, who had left a large amount of money to each grand child. We all pried away at him, trying to get him to open up more specifically about the turmoil at home, but he wasn't a lick his normal self. He seemed like an astronaut being reintroduced to Earth; it was a painful transition back to the horrors of reality.

Dave spent most of his first few days spread out across the pilled floral sofa, dispensing his fears in food and relenting from a move outdoors. He was always removed—but this week set a new precedent. The more he distanced himself, the more we became gravely concerned. His wallowing pity parties lasted most of the day, at which point he'd entertain the idea of dinner. For Dave, dinner was the most grand of all productions. Selecting what to eat, where to go, and even what we'd all wear, meant a great deal to him. As such, we allowed those choices to be entirely on his shoulders for the length of his stay. Sometimes it's the simple gestures that get people back on course.

This particular evening, Dave desired Mexican, so we drove three miles down the beach highway to the magnificent La Cocina. The restaurant was right up the road from the Beach Side summer kick off concert, which featured up and coming bands and was an altogether good time.

After a scrumptious Tex-Mex meal, in which we consumed hundreds of hand crafted chips and salsa, Stone suggested we grab an 18 pack from the corner stone. This was not so far off from Stone's greatest desire for our journey. He wanted to sit drunkenly, completely jolly on the beach, laughing away life's many injustices. Stone wanted to forget. But didn't we all? The curses of life outweighed the pros; and the cons swarmed and plagued the daylight hours until they submerged us all to our shallow night graves. Daylight breeds hopefulness as nighttime births desperation. A complex phenomenon, but one Stone, myself and all the other bleedings hearts came to know all too well.

Tensions had mounted each day Alec and Blythe did not connect again sexually. Blythe, Alec and Dave were tucked close together, victims of my coupe. Tonight was the night they might hash it out, I figured. She had a look on her face the entire day that told the world to back off.

We headed to the summer kick-off concert on the beach club patio, where a soulful southern rock band was playing to a crowd of 1,000 other young fools. Music tends to ratchet up the desire that we all have to be loved, conjuring emotions not often seen or felt. It often acts as an outlet for feelings to come spilling out.

Blythe approached Alec as we waited for the concert to begin on the huge patio lawn with the greenest grass I had ever seen. I did my best to overhear their exchange.

"Alec, I honestly need to know something," she pleaded.

"What's that?" Stone replied in a muted tone.

"Why am I here? Where is this going? I just, I feel like this is something different than with the other guys. You're so different." Forgive her pretty little heart, but that was the best way she could explain it; she was a simple gal. Though Stone knew that this conversation would occur, he did not quite anticipate it so soon. Her directness shocked him unexpectedly.

"I don't know what you want me to say, Blythe. You're a special person. I've enjoyed having you around, you know?" He used the expression you know when nothing else came to mind.

"Really? You don't know what to say?" Blythe did her best to stay emotionless. Their bodies tossed back and forth with a tension and angst only felt when two lovers are soon to be no longer. The push and pull, one desirous of more and another desirous of another, is an unparalleled emotional experience.

"Well yeah, I want you here," Stone continued. "It's just with Dave here, I'm not sure how to handle us," his voice trailing off. Stone spoke without realizing the hole he just plummeted down into. I could be one dumb son-of-a-bitch, but Stone dug holes like no other man I knew.

"Alec, he won't care. We're cousins, not siblings—not former lovers or something. Let's talk to him after the show if that's all you're worried about," she said. Her statements were firm and passion dripped off her vocal chords.

"Here's the thing... I just can't. I'm not really ready. And I don't know how to do this. We've been good friends for years. I don't think I can be with you right now. It's not about you, I swear. It's all about how fucked up I am on the inside. I'm still caught up recovering from my ex, Callie; that's why I sought this journey in the first place.... But seriously, if you hear anything I'm saying, please believe me when I tell you that you're an amazing girl," he stammered painfully.

Her face grew melancholic, and her energy to protest began to wane. His mind—for now—appeared to be as set as his last name.

68

"Why did you even bring me here then? You're pretty inconsiderate if you think the best way to get over a girl is to date and sleep with another one," she yelled, clearly frustrated and perturbed. She grabbed the case of beer and headed alone for the beach walkover. Alec would follow her she imagined; that's the way it always played out in the movies. But I knew better. There was no changing his mind. For Alec, the final chapter in their book had been written. The two former lovers headed in different directions. One thinking the other would chase after, but all Alec Stone ever knew how to do was run. My night, however, played out much differently. As the final chapter came to completion for Alec and Blythe, the first chapter of something exhilarating began for me.

Across Cobbled Alleys

Chapter 6

As Blythe and Stone diverted, Desi and I stood in the mass of college students, most of who were preparing for the concert by drinking wine out of red solo cups. Stone came back shortly, smiling but insincerely.

"Are you okay?" Desi asked sweetly.

"Of course. I'll be fine. I'm excited to hear this band you and Turner have talked so much about," he replied.

Not satisfied, Desi continued.

"Where's Blythe? Didn't she walk down to the beach with you?"

"It's nothing, no need to worry. She decided to spend some time alone to think about some things. I'll go look for her later if she doesn't come back soon," he assured.

"Well okay, I just hate the thought of her walking around here all alone," she said, turning toward me.

"Should I go look for her?"

"Nah, it's perfectly safe here. She probably just needs space. If she doesn't come back in an hour or so, then maybe you should go find her," I stated.

Seconds later, a beautiful creature emerged amidst the throngs of people. Standing in a lemon yellow tank top, which matched her sunshine smile, she waltzed toward us. The steam rose in the night and the onlookers' sported towels and bottled water to extinguish the 95-degree heat, ever present in Florida, even at night. Mary Kate approached hesitantly, a brunette friend in tow, and Desi waved them over. Desi introduced the girls as "MK" and "Chelsea," two gals she met that day wandering the beachside community at the local bookstore.

Stone looked to me excitedly to gauge my reaction. Knowing my affinity for girls with mile wide smiles, and being the world's best wingman, Alec positioned himself to my right, near the brunette.

"Dibs on Chelsea," he whispered.

I didn't reply. He could have Chelsea. My eyes were transfixed on MK and exiting the loneliness I had been harboring too long.

"Hey, I'm Turner..." I said, staring only into the small eyes of MK. The music began and it drowned out any noises that opposed it quickly. We dialogued and joked and she had a hope in her eyes that sparkled and expanded contagiously. All to my advantage, the soulful southern cooing of sweet music bled on loudly and allowed us to speak close, mouth to ear, skin grazed on skin and the emotional anticipation blossomed. The excitement of the night, of something new, blossomed with every movement from her lips.

"What do you love?" She asked confidently.

"What do you mean?" I asked her, surprised at how bold she was.

"I mean exactly what I said; what do you love?" Catching my bewilderment, she continued. "What do you love...about this band, Turner? They are absolutely amazing, your sister said you've seen them before," she giggled. She giggled like a hyena. She was quick on her feet. I liked that. I buckled over laughing and achieved creases around my mouth only a smile could contrive. It was rare for a girl to make me laugh like that. Probably beyond my sister, very few ever had.

"Yeah, we've seen them a time or two. They're absolutely electric when you see them live. What's not to love, MK?" I shot back, rapid fire.

"I mean, when you find something you love, I hope it's so clear that you cannot possibly deny it," spacing out my words delicately.

"I'm talking music, specifically this music, of course." I chimed in unnecessarily. It won't be the first time nor the last I say something stupid because I'm too damn nervous. My exterior was cool, but my insides were boiling over. Struggling with silence is my cross to carry, and I'll always struggle to exist in silence with those who I do not know well. The show ended and the music bled out mercilessly and I offered her a ride back to where she was staying. She agreed with a reply of "sure," and a smile.

"I'll catch up with you guys later," I said to Desi and Alec, who were heading with Chelsea to The Blitz, a local bar.

The drive home across Phillips Inlet lasted five forever-long minutes. She laughed and chirped and challenged—she was

72

majestic. It wasn't long before my wonder led me to consider how many gentlemen had found her equally majestic before me. "I'd like to see you again Mary Kate," my words stammered like a drunken teenager. "We could have dinner or coffee," but anything would have sufficed.

"That sounds awesome; let's do that sometime," she was nonchalant. We neared her door before I knew what had even happened and she kissed my blush stained cheek without speaking.

"Goodnight," echoed as she ran inside her ocean side abode. "Goodnight MK," I said, only the falling stars above listening.

Compelling, those miniscule feelings can rob a heart blind. I'd digressed to being an unintentionally selfish man due to my fear of losing control. I was weary with experience and using each muster I could to convey confidence and general happiness. Knowing my mission was to be an accent, a light, to the beautiful universe, I kept challenging myself to love someone. When you *love* all people, and only few love you back to the same extent, with the same passionate bleeding heart love, it can be the wearing of cheap, rubber tires on a gravel road; one of the most heartbreaking things in this life.

I arrived home early in the morning hours to find Alec Stone spread eagle on the wood floor, dead to the world. "Quite a night, my friend," I whispered, even if he couldn't hear. In the shuffle of time when a boy is wrapped up in youthful lust with a mesmerizing girl, I'd lost Stone, Chelsea, and Desi. Much to my surprise, all three were passed out in the condo. Desi happily asleep in the living room; Chelsea oddly resolving the kitchen as her dwelling place for the evening. I wondered where in the world Blythe was. I didn't bother looking, very much engrossed in my own world.

I scrubbed the dirty pans in the enormous sink passionately, chuckling to myself. Nothing seemed too large, or too difficult, and I smiled quietly too, hoping to allow Chelsea more slumber. I rinsed quickly, placing the dishes on a green and white crocheted towel. It was the only dishtowel in the house.

Elusive as it may be, I had an over the moon, stars, aloft in the singing sky feeling in my chest, and I desired nothing as much as to fall into a dream—reliving the beautiful evening God had hand assembled for me; or for us, maybe. I put on Valtari, the Sigur Ros album and it walked me slowly down a candle lit, cobblestone path in my mind toward sleep. As I stared at the ceiling, it was like a light switch had been turned on. I could still do this. I only had to wait, remain patient and let God work his miracles. I whispered goodnight to the heavens. It was a truly good night.

***

"My freakin' head," Stone moaned as he finally emerged from his bedroom cave and entered into my room. It wasn't the

74

way either of us wanted to wake up.

"What'd you end up doing last night?" I asked rolling from my resting place, but refusing to open my eyes all the way.

"I think Chelsea," he mused.

"Wait—What?" I replied puzzled.

"You asked me what I did last night. Really, you mean whom did I do last night. But yeah, I did Chelsea."

"Damn Alec! How do you get yourself into this shit?" I asked so half-heartedly that he knew it did not elicit a response. His typical rants predictably began with three simple words, the ultimate qualifier: "Here's the thing... Chelsea is hot, she's witty and she has good taste in men, obviously. How could I say no?" We both chuckled, me as the master who just had my guide dog show me its catch, Stone as the victorious young man with a trophy.

"What ever happened with Blythe? Did she ever come back and find y'all last night?"

Every ounce of blood drained from his already pale face. The Florida sunshine had yet to do him any assistance on his ever pale-white skin. A number of four letter expletives followed.

"Is she still in her room? Still asleep?" Stone pursed his lips.

"The shower actually," I interjected.

"Shit! But then where's Chelsea?" Alec Stone panicked as I watched his mind sprint in an Olympic race, running in last place.

"Oh, she's in the kitchen," I said neglecting to mention her unconscious state.

"Mother of Moses! She's just settling in making waffles or something?" His distraught covered his cheeks, which were burgundy.

"I think pancakes, actually," I prodded.

"Jacobs, come on man! This is not the time for jokes. Not the effing time!"

"Relax Alec, Chelsea is very much cashed out still sleeping. Just like I was before you barged in here," I gasped for breath, laughing through each word.

With that, Stone disappeared, the garage door below my room rattled seconds later. And as I stared from the sliding door, my car whipped up the road. His acceleration could be heard the whole length of the street. I pulled my iPhone from my wall charger and sent him a short and direct text.

"What do you want me to do?"

In the past, for those outside his inner circle, it was nearly impossible to see Alec's fear. His confidence was at times blinding; but even Alec was raised fearfully. We are all prone to fear to some extent.

His Father, Allen, had an addictive personality. He was a gambler, and dice roller, much like his son, but conversely, Allen never seemed to garner much success. He was a person who was listless and lost, and when he wasn't busy feeding his alcoholism and other supplementary addictions, his time was spent away from his only son, Alec. Jan, his wife and Alec's mother, saved Alec from the same path as her husband. A mother's love can overcome all shackles. It can reduce nearly all fear.

Still, the younger Stone, a proud and stubborn individual, was always at war with the sins that were built into his bloodstream. Deep in the past something within him snapped— something didn't make sense about the vast glowing emptiness of our human flesh. He was ultra cognizant of the world's shortcomings, yet he lived life with a zeal that did not worry about tomorrow. His mentality said "live for today and today alone." He didn't leave anything on his plate, in any circumstance, ever. To not squeeze every last minute out of each piping hot day was the only authentic sin to Alec Stone. And so, this as a benchmark, he rarely sinned.

An hour passed and Alec was still missing in action. Thinking on my feet, I asked Blythe to go on a bike ride. She obliged, sluggishly. I knew I needed to get her out of the house. "Where's Alec?" She asked, strapping on her Chaco sandals. "The grocery store, I think."
"Huh? Why? He is so weird sometimes. Who just up and goes to the grocery store?" She smiled naively and threw two large camelback bottles spilling over with cool water in the bike's basket to negate the 90-degree heat. Though I had no desire to bike, I needed to ensure that Blythe and Chelsea did not cross

paths. I sent a short to Desi.

"Mission get rid of Chelsea commence."

She replied almost instantaneously: "Who the hell is Chelsea?" She had probably engaged in a bit too much Chardonnay last night. While riding my Schwinn bike with no hands for the first time in years, I wrote: "One of the girls you introduced us to last night. She's in our kitchen. Please help keep her occupied. Better yet, get her out of the house if you can."

"Oh shit. Alright, I'll go upstairs in a few minutes. Need to throw up again first," she replied.

Letting my mind be free as my hands, I realized Blythe to be fairly enjoyable one on one. I pondered the fact I never gave her a fair chance; she was undeniably genuine. I felt guilty for writing her off too soon and not getting to know her properly. "Blythe, I'm definitely glad you're here with us. I've sort of wanted to ask you what made you want to come on such a whim? I mean, you hardly know any of us after all," I said, attempting to sound casual.

She giggled, but soon became semi-serious.

"Mainly for Alec. He's different than any guy I've ever known. He's intriguing and intoxicating and talkative and exciting. He never sits still; when all of you are together, it's like this frenetic sense of energy buzzing like a telephone wire. I like all of that. But, I also came for the same reason you came. Just looking for some semblance of purpose more than working 50 hours a week

78

at a job that I hate. She sounded so sure of herself.

"Alec is my closest friend in the world, Blythe, you know that. He can definitely be all of those things. His heart is legitimately well intentioned. But because I know him so well, I also know his shortcomings, too," I stated.

She cut me off before I could say more.

"What are you getting at, Turner? You don't have to use caveats, just be straightforward with me. God knows I deserve that much in all this craziness," she stated.

I was stunned at her word choice, her abrupt change in tone, and looked around befuddled momentarily.

She was right, she deserved each and every one of those things. Sadly, life is not always delivered as deserved. But today, easy or not, I had to be fair with her. Summing up courage and wiping a mountain of sweat out from under my discolored and worn Florida State ball cap, I gathered up all of the courage I had.

"I'm just not so sure he has the right feelings for you. And you deserve someone who really wants to get to know all of you, Blythe. You really deserve poetic, life changing, and heart attacking love. Maybe Alec's just not the one to provide that to you. He has been so lost lately. Mad, insane, confused and so quick to run away from his problems. You don't need to put up with all of that bullshit. Who wants to always be wondering if the person they are falling for is falling for them too?"

I felt bad talking about my best friend is such coarse terms.

Her hazel eyes filled with waterfalls and her face marooned, embarrassed. We were both worn mightily with shame. Blythe, in her innermost soul was somber and sad for chasing the always-moving Alec, and I felt the same emotions for allowing him to break any of her heart. She was old enough to make her own decisions, we both knew that, but in a twisted way, I felt a sense of responsibility. No girl deserved to cry like the rain.

"You really think that? He's just gone off the deep end and I am caught in the middle of the mess?" She squeaked, her voice failing to create distinguishable words. She spoke with the deep-rooted sting of pain that only unrequited love created.

"I could be wrong, but I don't think that I am to be honest," I shrugged.

One of life's greatest conundrums is who will open their gates for us to gain access to their whole heart; and maybe more importantly, who will close those gates off to all other possibilities? Alec, for all the wonderful things he was, just wasn't in a place where he could close his gate off to others. His personality was to spread the wealth, literally and metaphorically, and him committing to any one individual, no matter how lovely she might be, was more asinine than realistic. But even so, girl after girl fell under his cheeky grin and spell.

"Just get me home, Turner. I want to lie down," she stated explicitly.

80

"You got it, Blythe," I replied as we rushed back toward the beach house.

My phone buzzed, it was Desi finally letting me know that she had not made it from the bathroom and couldn't locate Chelsea.

"Where the flip did she go?" I replied, texting her back quickly.

"Not sure. I'm still sick as a dog, but I haven't heard her anywhere in the house," Desi replied.

"Okay, well is Alec back? Blythe is demanding we go back to the beach house right now," I wrote.

"I honestly don't know, but I think I heard the garage door open. Maybe he's here somewhere."

As we got closer and closer to the house, I couldn't stop my big mouth from flooding out unnecessary information in hopes of negating the World War that I assumed we would be walking into.

"So there's this other girl, Chelsea, who might be at the house right now. She came back with us after you and Alec got into that disagreement last night. She's just a friend of ours, nothing to be concerned about," I said, notably awkwardly.

"Um okay? Why are you telling me about her then?"

"It's just that I didn't want you to read into things, or assume something happened, that's all. I didn't want you to think she hooked up with any of us or anything," I declared.

She rolled her eyes and looked at me agitated, and said nothing but a simple "okay," as we pulled up to the beach house and saw

Alec Stone sitting on the porch sipping on a beer.

We rounded the stairs, one after the other, and walked into the living room. Before any further preparation could be accomplished, or foibles potentially squashed, our eyes were drawn to Chelsea, who was sitting proudly on the couch in Alec Stone's button down shirt, wearing the same shorts she wore the night before eating a bowl of oatmeal. Alec's two lovers' eyes met and telepathically something was amiss, and the girls seemed in tune to the catastrophe at hand.

"Hey, I'm Chelsea. Who's your friend, Turner?"

Before I could speak, Blythe interjected.

"Hey, I'm Blythe, Alec's girlfriend," and with a shutter every step felt frozen in time.

"You're his what? Turner, what is she talking about? He took me home last night and didn't say anything about a girlfriend," Chelsea said innocently.

I looked over at Blythe, who looked somewhere between Mike Tyson and Satan enraged, and was scared to open my mouth for fear of being a target for her fury.

"Hey Alec? Come on down here," I yelled to the porch.

He must've known what was coming, because he inched his way toe-by-toe, sauntering too slowly down to the living area.

"What's up guys? It's a freaking beautiful day out there today," he gestured as he rounded the corner.

"Beautiful day? What in the hell are you talking about you

asshole? You have literally lost your mind," Blythe shrieked and out of nowhere, she sprung at him like a lion devouring its prey. His knees buckled, catching him by surprise as they toppled over and fell down the last three stairs in unison to the floor. Smacks could be heard as Blythe shockingly began using her dainty hand to slap Stone in the face repeatedly like a crack addict trying to obtain their next fix.

"Stop! Seriously just stop already! Get the fuck off of me! I've never hit a girl, and I'm not going to start now unless you don't get off me," he choked out, covering his face with his hands.

"You're a bastard! I knew this whole thing was too good to be true," Blythe shrieked miserably, while crying and pulling her body to a seated position on his torso as he lay flat like a surfboard to the ground.

"What is she doing here and why did you think I wouldn't find out?" Blythe was manic.

"It's all my fault. I really screwed this whole thing up. But let me explain, please," Alec began.

"What is there to explain? I can see her right here, in your shirt, clearly you slept with her, too," she cried.

"Um, no he didn't. I'm not some kind of slut. We just hung out and chilled last night," Chelsea spoke up.

"You shut your damn mouth. You have no right to even talk to me," Blythe yelled nastily.

"Blythe, knock it off, don't talk to her that way. She didn't even know anything," I added, realizing I had further implicated my already terribly embroiled friend.

"I didn't mean to hurt anyone. Blythe, I'm so sorry, I really am. I have to be honest, I don't think you and I are meant to be together and after our fight last night, I met Chelsea and we really connected. You know you're not my girlfriend! We just started talking and I already feel like it's not right between us. I seriously suck for how this happened, but we're not good for each other and you know it," he said, sympathetically.

Blythe looked at Chelsea, who looked altogether bewildered, and got up off of Alec Stone.

"You're a bastard. A full of shit, no good liar just like the rest of them. If you knew we weren't meant to be together, why didn't you tell me not to come to Florida?" and she dusted herself up before anyone could get another word in edgewise.

"I don't, I don't know. I really blew it and I'm sorry you're hurt," Alec added.

"You're sorry I'm hurt? Okay, I'm done. I'm done being here. I need to go home right now," simple and powerful were her words. I readily complied.

"I'm so sorry, Blythe. I should know better than this," Alec said as she departed, but she didn't care to hear him.

I knew I'd never see Blythe again when she entered the taxi. Her sundress flowing in the wind, suitcase stuffed until the zippers wanted to burst, large Vera Bradley turquoise and amethyst bag hanging low, and one incredibly sunken heart.

"I'm sorry, too, Blythe. No one should have to put up with what happened in there. It's not fair at all. And seriously, one day, you're going to make someone incredibly, incomprehensibly happy," exaggerating just ever so slightly but that was all right. She forced a smile. Sometimes a small lie covers up huge holes in another's heart. Though honesty is critically important, and was built into my DNA before I can remember, sometimes little white lies can serve as a Band-Aid to bless broken hearts.

"Someday, I hope I feel that way. Sorry if I lost my cool in there. I'm not crazy, you know? He deserved every last bit of someone standing up to him, though. I don't think any girl ever has," she mumbled.

"Not really. No one has ever really had to," I replied.

"Well Turner, thank you. I know this must have been a miserable position to be put in, but you were great, so thanks," and she blew a kiss and her hair ran with the coastal winds and in one fast move, she was gone. God love her, God bless her. Innocence and insanity coexisting perfectly within her honey heart, I hoped all of the fear would be driven out of it. I prayed to God out loud. "Let her find her happiness, Lord. It's hers to be captured after all." But isn't it out there for me too? And for all those that I know and love? I hoped with all of my heart it was on the horizon for all of us.

Across Cobbled Alleys

Chapter 7

Soul searching in the moonlit foggy summer night, violet skies brushed by God himself—this trumped any desire for money. But like all things, even our listless wandering—free of debts to this juncture—had to come to an end.

Admittedly, Stone and I had not truly estimated the cost of our endeavors on the road. Stone's parents, who were shockingly not upset that Alec had departed town, weren't admittedly thrilled with our usage of their credit card to cover the cost of our gas and food. We had little money left to our names, and like other individuals in tourist towns, turned to the retail job market in hope of making a quick buck. After a handful of applications, pointless questions about what address we were living at and our past employment, we were able to sell our dynamic duo to a wealthy boot salesman in the extremely affluent vacation district of Beach Side. The owner, Chet, was married to an overweight debutante, but was clearly gay and uncomfortable in his own skin. He was in his early 50s, but dressed in ripped jeans and skintight tee shirts like he was like in his 20s. He flicked his wrist when he talked, giggled frequently and had no filter when it came to fashion or political topics. He wore a thick layer of gel in his hair and his eyebrows were waxed and sharply pointed at the brow bone. He delegated sales and stocking responsibilities to both of us, and we were to assist the ladies that worked in the store in retrieving hard to reach boxes in the back room. I didn't mind the work, I always liked to have a project going, but Alec despised it. He was emaciated and distraught over Blythe's sudden disappearance, and was quickly losing touch with reality. Since the day she left, he spent hours wallowing around the home in his oversized blue and red plaid sleep pants, shirtless, drinking beer from sun up to sun down. It was as pathetic as I ever had ever seen him. Shaken and unkempt, he looked old. Stone had never looked a day above 17 in his life. His face was nearly wrinkle free—he was difficult to distinguish from your common high school student, but on this day, he looked nearly double his age.

Meanwhile, Chelsea was falling under his spell, even if he wasn't trying to make her fall a bit—taking care of him and waiting on his every beck and call. She only wanted to further know the mysteries that comprised Alec Stone. How did he become the charismatic disaster that she saw before her eyes?

Her eager desire appeared to cause greater resistance from Stone. Why must relationships always go this way? How perplexing is it that one person can be skylight high, head over heels falling in love and the other can be totally disinterested, like a fresh wicked candle with no desire to be set ablaze? While Chelsea was ready to burn away, Stone burnt his final dollars on two bottles of Sauvignon Blanc. Fear crept into his eyes, and I knew even whilst very much on this important journey searching for his purpose, he still felt lost. I thought I was lost, but soon realized I wasn't in too bad a place after all. I wanted so badly to help my best friend out of this slump, but he didn't want out just yet. Isn't that the most complex thing with the saddest of souls? They want to wallow. Worry is a friend to no one, but Stone let it sustain him since Callie had left him. Even 1,000 miles away from home with a beautiful girl on his arm, fear didn't depart.

Getting a job, which required us to work a minimum of four days per week, was essential to turning Alec's far-out ship back toward shore. Monotony has a strange correlation to stability. The job was in fact Alec's lifeboat. And we paddled together, because one person cannot properly direct a lifeboat. It was a multiple person affair that led the sorrowful back to the hopeful shore. I knew it wouldn't be an overnight fix. I prayed it would be short, though. He had suffered too long.

It was Saturday and we'd worked nine straight days. It was nearly summertime and going to work was the last damn thing we wanted to do. This was time for meeting new women, lounging, basking in sunshine skies and immersing our souls deep in beautiful music; it was not the time for hour upon hour of menial work, pushing overpriced boots to snobby middle-aged housewives.

Two of our co-workers were continually missing in action, one recently divorced and in some serious misery, the other caught up in the bottle. Alec and I picked up extra shifts in lieu of our co-workers on the regular. After a certain period of doing so, there was a disgruntled tension boiling one thousand degrees hot. Resentment, like mold, grew more prevalent each day.

"I need a break from my break, Stone," I bellyached.

"You got that right. I can't even remember what day of the week it is. All I know full and well is that regardless of the day, our butts will be up here, working," he sighed.

"Let's take a day off," he suggested.

"And say what? We both got the flu at the same time?" I retorted.

"It's plausible. We do live together after all," he smiled.

"Fine, but you're calling in for the both of us, buddy."

"Done deal. I'll fake flirt with Chet and get this thing taken care of," and he walked to the porch to call the store's owner.

Running on empty, we needed a day off from work. I didn't feel that bad about lying to Chet. He was an ass, always running his finger on any part of the floor there was dust, and making an example out of anyone who didn't straighten all 2,500 hangers in the door. To boot, I always felt like he was creepily checking me out when I moved things around the store, bending down and reaching up to place items just the way he wanted. But desperate enough for money, I continued to work there, knowing the job was entirely temporary.

What we chose to do with our day off honestly didn't matter. It was more about having the choice to determine a sliver of time in our existence again. To drift away as the pack of seagulls cast overhead, and soar higher or lower or to sit on the bluff by the bay for as long as was so desired. Time was not our constraint; we chose where we wanted to be and how long we wanted to be there. It was the most freeing feeling there is on Mother Earth.

Walking at waters edge, half past one, seeing the sand bubble beneath my every footstep, I sensed that God had our lives planned perfectly. My father's voice echoed in my head. "Having the power to control one's own destiny, and the power over your own time. That, my son, means everything. And at the end of your life, it'll be the only thing you want more of: time."

Our first checks were handsome, and I decided to spend the majority of the check planning a date with Mary Kate, who I had only seen sparingly since our initial encounter. Even in those brief moments, she could dialogue with the best of them. She could goof off, or be serious. And that smile. A smile only an Earthly angel might possess. While I was bumble bee busy procuring things for the date later that night, Stone stocked his cart with only the *essentials*: Heineken, lunch meat, cold medicine to help him sleep, peaches and a bottle of wine. I've never known a man who enjoyed peaches quite so much. I tried to convince him to go on a double date with Mary Kate, Chelsea and I but he scoffed at it.

As the date approached, I realized it'd been nearly a year

since I was this genuinely excited to see another human being. I was so fallible and off my game after things fell apart with Jez that I had been living very reluctant to show my true colors that were exploding out of my insides to anyone. It scared me greatly for the first time in my life. My open book style of living had hit a brick wall.

Sparks bubbled in my veins and my arteries pumped the richest, thickest blood concoction through me as she neared my house. I decided to cook her dinner, which I'd seldom tried; I sat the table with brand-new place settings, down to the napkins, and violet-colored plates with large yellow polka dots on them. I made chicken linguini, and undercooked the noodles dramatically. She only said how "wonderful" it tasted. I blushed like a schoolboy.

"So how do you like going to school up at Auburn?" I asked, breaking the silence.

"I really like it. I'm part of a sorority, so that keeps me super busy," she smiled.

"Where did you go to school, Turner? You just graduated right?"

"Yeah, I went to a college up in Michigan at a small, Christian college about two hours from home. That's where I became best friends with Alec, actually. We'd known one another for a really long time, but it was at college that we found out just how much alike we are," I smiled.

"That's so awesome. Sometimes I wish I went to a small college where I could establish closer relationships with people. Going to a huge school like Auburn, it can be challenging to make close friendships. That's the main reason I joined a sorority. It makes the big college feel much smaller," she said. She was so elegant as we spoke. Her hands flowed happily and she rubbed her right arm with her left hand.

"I haven't been on a date in awhile," she confessed, surprising me.

"You haven't? I've got to admit that I haven't either," I stated with relief.

"No way? You put on a pretty damn good date, Turner Jacobs," she said smiling from head to toe.

"Really? I just like to take girls on dates that they deserve. And let's be honest, you justify one amazing date," I said, stumbling over my words.

I could only smile. I knew I could be nervous, sweaty and even awkward at times, but I was ecstatic. I was on top of the world just knowing that I could still do this. I still had it.

Did God give me a date with a girl so kind I could hardly sit still or be calm or a normal variety of myself? Early in any dating situation, men are indubitably blind to what is actually going on. We live too much inside our own heads, hardly able to acknowledge what is occurring around us in the actual universe. If there's a beautiful woman in front of us, we are lost in a one-way maze where our eyes only see her.

And so we ate, swallow—pause—swallow— nearly choke to death, the way one eats on a first formal date. I've never been able to put my finger on it, but initially, eating a meal with another person is horribly obtuse. You begin rambling and your food gets ice cold; you try to ask questions while they are awkwardly chewing. And the beat goes on until completion, with one shared ultimate goal: will this person across from me ever love me? Will I love them? But we dance the dance, play the game and allow things to "naturally" occur over a more elongated period of time.

**

After dinner, we walked 100 yards to the beach and sunk our feet into the salty white sands of Beachside. I wanted it to be simple, but memorable. I wanted it to create a lasting impression in her mind so that when she thought of her time living in Beach Side, she thought of me. Stone, who owed me from the Blythe fiasco, lit grocery store fireworks off from behind the brush as we sat on the seashore, lying on a beach towel. They blazed the sky masterfully, exploding as we spoke.

We tossed, turned, and became sticky and moist, results of prolonged exposure to the saccharine summer ocean air while our jaws ran marathons. Words, phrases, sentences, fragments swam the seashore and the orange man in the moon kept our thoughts between the three of us. Listening was always a challenge for me, but MK's words weighed on me like pillars; I heard every single syllable of every single word.

Pea size eyes couldn't disguise any of her heart, and my brain waves repeated, "don't screw this up." What were these foreign emotions? Why can't I breathe? Am I talking too much? Not enough? How's my hair? Wow, she looks absolutely incredible. I want to kiss her. Does she want to kiss me? What in the hell do I do right now? What do I do with my hands?

Lost somewhere between wanting to place my wounded heart in her hands and wondering if this was as absurd an action as my conscious brain knew it was, loneliness makes for a weak human being. Put two in the same room, and all of the sudden, one latches on and sometimes the other person does too. Other times, the other person only feels lonelier than they felt before.

And so we waltzed, hands intertwined, to her car. Cliché, much who I am, I didn't want her to go. My insides yearned for her to stick to me a little longer. Her sheen skin rubbing on mine, what else could a man ever want? Did she feel even a sliver of the same? Was I getting ahead of myself, thinking about all the wonderful adventures we could share? My hard heart told me to slow down. If I've learned any single thing in my life, someone always leaves. Always. The real question is not if, but when? Who will give up first?

Scraping the negative particles from my thoughts, an overwhelming tremble ran full steam down the tresses of my spine and overcame me. Was there genuine interest or simply loneliness that brought us here together, tonight? Not even MK wanted to admit the fact that I was visiting Florida for a short time. There would be no love affair, just a memory left sprinkled amongst the stars in the sky of our minds. So we hugged goodbye, I kissed her cheek and we called it a night. I hoped desperately, the way all youthful lovers do, there could be many more.

I went to sleep elated. As a new sun rose the next morning, just as it had every day of my life to date, I beamed with a smile. My heart felt lighter as I daydreamed about the night before. It felt straight out of a movie. I should've kissed her. Next time, I'm going in, I told myself. Regardless of what didn't happen, I grinned from ear to ear. All provided by the validation of a pretty girl from Dothan, Alabama.

Across Cobbled Alleys

Chapter 8

Hours ticked off the clock as I dreamt of a second date with Mary Kate. Time always moves at a snails pace when you so desperately want it to speed up. Conversely, time slips away all too quickly when we hope for it to slow down so that we might embrace it like a southern summer night. Sitting up until ungodly hours, which I've always found to be a weird saying since all hours belong to God anyway, I watched NPR videos on my YouTube account. It was one of the only entirely peaceful rituals that I had: and one I repeated often. I had the house to myself, candles illuminated the living room and the lampshades were hanging over light bulbs seldom used. Nestled with my nose in a book, and the sunset painting me happy and relaxed, I dozed on and off. As soon as I nodded off once and for all, my phone buzzed itself off the counter and the screen illuminated with the face of Alec Stone.

"What're you doing still out? Where is everybody?" I questioned what insane things they might be up to.

"It's Dave. Something fucking terrible has happened. I don't even know what exactly but he's at the hospital," his breath was heavy on the line.

"What do you mean the hospital? Which hospital?" I asked flabbergasted.

"The Emerald Coast Hospital on Blakeley Road. How quick can you be here?" He asked.

"I'm already gone," I shouted, heart tightly clenched.

"I'll explain what I know when you get here," Stone shouted and the line clicked.

My saliva glands felt like they weren't producing anything and I was drinking my own spit like bottled water as I raced to Emerald Coast Hospital with the fear of the unknown. The fear of the unknown always trumps the fear of the known. I wondered if Dave had been in a car wreck. I wondered if he had broken bones or a dislocated shoulder or bruising. I shut off my wondering brain, and raced to the hospital.

As I entered, there sat Stone, Desi and Chelsea, with Dave in the hospital electric blue glow. "I hate hospitals," kept repeating in my head. As if the pungent odor wasn't enough, people sat draped in worry and malicious pain, all well tucked behind a billion dollar brick façade.

Twisted thing really. People can't afford health care yet American builds bigger and better hospitals all over this country. Somewhere in the confusion, mankind can't receive proper care without necessary insurance and disgusting sums of money changing hands. "It all costs something." But I contest that it costs nothing near the egregious amount demanded for it.

Alec began before I could open my mouth as I strolled in. "Dave tried to kill himself," he shook his head in utter disbelief.

I gasped, though I had been worried about Dave for some time. I never conceived it was this bad, though.

"Yeah, he took a cocktail of prescription pills. Had a note in his jeans pocket and everything. Thankfully, Chelsea heard him throwing up and became concerned and called 911," he rubbed her arm softly, nurturing. I wasn't even sure why Chelsea had been with them or where they had been—but this was not the time to concern myself with love affairs.

I'd been struggling for sleep, sweet and far off, and was accidentally higher than a skyscraper on Ambien. A miserable, stomach swirling, purple monster causing hallucinogen when not effective, I couldn't remember anything from the night except arriving at the hospital. I was groggy as ever. I could hardly recount how I got to standing in the waiting room.

"So, is he in a coma? What's going on? Can we see him yet?" I rattled off, concerned.

Stone rubbed his chin with his forefinger and thumb slowly. Chelsea fought off tears, looking distraught with angst.

"He's resting actually. Doctors said the stomach pumping process took the energy right out of him and that he needed time. No visitors for now. I'm not sure what I would say in the first place," Stone said gravely.

I nodded solemnly.

"So, he's going to be okay, right? Are we taking him back to the beach house or does he want to head back to Michigan?" So

98

many thoughts began tearing through my mind and even though it was not the time, they leapt out past my tongue from my mouth.

"We don't know much yet. They think he'll be fine but he is on a 48 hour psych watch for the suicide attempt and I guess we'll go from there. How the hell did we all miss this, Turner?"

"I don't know. I feel like we should've picked up on this a long time ago, man. Fuck, I feel like the worst person in the world right now," I declared.

"Me too. Don't worry about this whole thing. No one is to blame. We're going to figure this out with the doctors here and get a plan of action together," Stone said.

Seeing Stone take control of a problematic situation was refreshing. He often left these types of scenarios for others to decipher and solve. The entire time this conversation occurred, there sat Chelsea at his side with her left hand slumped across his lower back. It was cute and perplexing altogether, but I was not of sound mind to read into the peculiar happenings between Alec and Chelsea.

"I'll call his Mother," Desi interjected from across the room.

"Please don't," Alec and I said in instantaneous unison.

"Why the hell not? She needs to know what is going on with her only son!" Desi demanded passionately.

"Not yet, it's too soon. His mother would die just thinking about this. She'd crumble into pieces. Why worry her further? Let's wait 48 hours and go from there," Stone remarked.

"She was petrified that he even traveled here to see us all alone. I can't imagine what she'd say if she knew about the extent of what happened," I added.

Suicide needs no displacement of blame, but we all wondered if any of it could be attributed to Dave's conservative, strict up bringing. He couldn't so much as breathe out of turn on Sunday—unless in the confines of a church. The hallowed church ground, at times oddly ominous and shadow laden as to illustrate the pervasive judgment of the outside world, provided the sinner a veil of comfort and sorrow and exacerbated guilt so strong in one's soul—it couldn't be severed. That is, until Monday rolled around again.

His family was involved in the community; outwardly they were a terrific family much like most in the Rochester area. Often though, they squandered their evenings after dark judging the decisions of others in their suburban, lantern lit neighborhood and found a self-righteous pleasure in their involvement in various religious organizations. The intrinsically negative, psychologically encompassing upbringing that Dave had been subjected to for twenty-three years would have driven even the sane to the threshold of insanity.

The backwards confusion of Dave's emotional rollercoaster that we had stumbled upon was becoming increasingly bewildering and bizarre. In the past, I'd been down sad, and sour, my ship sunk to be eaten by the bottom feeders, and yet I'd never be capable of taking my own breathe from my lungs. I would find any form of therapy I could to deflect the fragmented shards of pain from my own heart, while attempting to understand the grace that God had given me. He gave me more than I knew what to do with. I wanted desperately to understand it.

How could this be happening to a man who appeared to have an outwardly close connection to the Lord? It makes sense—life can beat you up—but how could it have gotten this far off track with all of us underneath the same damned roof, not willing to acknowledge it? I was ashamed with myself. I was usually less self-absorbed and more centered on all of the relationships I was blessed with. For some reason, my own confusion with life was taking its toll and I had let one of my dearest friends fall further into a pit without noticing. If he didn't survive, I knew I would never forgive myself. I wondered in the pit of my stomach if any of the others had seen this coming. I wondered if Alec harbored any of the same feelings of guilt that I couldn't escape.

At last, we were allowed to enter his room, though only one at a time. Desi suggested that I go first. Without a beat, I jumped up off the stiff hospital chair and headed for his room.

As I rounded the corner of the room, I first saw his arms, IV laden and his hand yellow and jaundice-like. I grabbed his hand hesitantly. It was so sweaty and salty. Nonetheless, I couldn't let go. The devilish glow of electric hospital light couldn't betide Dave.

After a heated discussion within my own brain to withhold my emotion, I kissed his forehead and decided to leave him alone for now. Stone followed my steps to the heavy hallway, and came near my ear in three swift steps.

"I hate to say it. I don't want to even go there, but seriously, something is peculiar with this whole thing, don't you think?"

"Just what it is—well, that I don't know yet," his face glistened with sweat. He glanced up and down the hallway with anxiety present in his eyes.

"Come on Alec. Seriously? This isn't the time for you to go all J.Edgar Hoover. I'll agree he's been acting strangely...a fraction of his typical self even, but that doesn't mean there is anything abnormal going on here. Other than the sheer fact he was so upset he wanted to end his life..." I exasperated a meek breath.

"You may be right, Jacobs. I just feel eerie about the whole thing. I really felt like he was making progress," Stone said.

"What the hell signs of progress are you talking about? Neither of us was giving him enough of our time. Don't you feel at all responsible for not helping him rehabilitate here, Alec? I don't know how I could miss all of these signs," I managed.

102

"Me? No! Why would I feel responsible for this?" He said, fuming. "Look, I hate with all my heart this happened, but this—this whole thing isn't our fault. It's not our fault in the slightest and we all need to get that thought through our heads right now," I replied.

I tried to show agreement, taking a passive approach, after seeing his face deepen to a shade of August red with anger. "You're probably right. I need to get back to bed. Are you up for staying here?"

"Yeah, I think I'll stay. Just in case anything happens," Stone stated matter of fact.

"Let me know Alec," I said.

"Of course," Stone complied.

The medicine made my head swirl so much that my brown leather shoes hit the hospital stairwell, spinning, and I left with my words still floating inside the crusted walls of floor three, building C at Emerald Coast Hospital with shoes untied.

***

Blythe had left. Desi was increasingly distant and seemed restless. Dave was hospitalized. Stone and I were born adventurers with wild fire in our hearts like Magellan or Christopher Columbus, hell bent on discovering things unseen and not stopping until the desire to search wore off. I kept contemplating packing up, putting all of my things in bags and running away. Maybe even running back home. Because ultimately, running becomes exponentially easier the more often one does it. But why run away so soon? Callie's wedding was right around the corner. I knew I had to stick around, if at all possible, because Alec would need the best version of me I could conjure up to get through that day.

As I looked down, a small piece of paper in my cup holder caught my eye. In colorful turquoise blue ink on a three by three business card was her full name and ten-digit phone number. Mary Kate Jones. 334-252-7979. And like that business card, small in stature was the glimmer of hope that remained in seeing her once again. My lonely fingers dialed her number. There was no point in leaving things left unsaid. No matter that she'd been ignoring me for over a week. Why give any situation less than your absolute best? It was embedded too deeply within my veins to give every situation my utmost.

In the past, I had left places because I was too scared to stay. No intrepid minded adventurer would ever want others to be aware of that. So, facing facts that only I needed to know, if I left the coastal beach town, it was due primarily to the bone-clenching fear that surrounded love and loss. Once we give up our brains demand to be dependent on another human being, we risk the complex puzzle that lies within our heart. No denying it is a phenomenon that cannot be explained easily.

Dave's situation made me ponder life so differently, on so many levels. Always two steps ahead and gaining momentum at

104

superficially expedited rates, why could no one slow me down? My mind ran—marathon distance and at a 100-meter dash pace—and I did all I could to keep my balance. I whipped into the driveway, directly off of highway 30-A and coasted into the garage seamlessly. My left hand clicked the lock button as an old habit as soon as I exited from behind the tinted windows.

The mounting stress due to Dave's suicide attempt was tortuous on my conscious. I needed desperately to hit the sheets for a night of legitimate slumber. As I lay there, watching time ebb and flow, I fell in and out of slumber for five hours. The contours of Dave's sickness and sadness stole sleep from me. I already felt the need to return to him pulsing within my body. No, you're higher than a cloud, Turner. Go to sleep. Sleep off this terrible feeling and go tomorrow when you're feeling of sound mind, I fought within myself. Stay in bed. Maybe if you lie silently, this will all disappear. It didn't, of course.

Too much time ticked off the clock and I had not been able to go fall asleep. I knew it was time to go back to Emerald Coast Hospital. Dave needed me now and I was damn well going to be there for him in his moment of need, even if it meant exhaustion. Exhaustion was a small price to pay for the true love of a friend.

Just a handful of hours ago I couldn't stand the sight, the sound, and the dying demoralization that rose like a plume around Dave's agonizing room.

Dave was sickly and drained to his nothingness; his gaunt face looked woefully depressed and I pictured it like a photograph I memorized. Getting back behind the wheel, I drove like a mad man to get to his bedside.

I entered the room slowly, and could hear the hum of the air conditioner and drone of Conan O'Brien on re-run. It was Dave's all-time favorite program. His ocean water blue eyes waved me over and I pulled a heavy, uncomfortable chair close to the bed. I remember wishing the right words would arrive to me by sheer fate or telepathy. Instead, I simply spoke the first words I could manage.

"Dave, what happened man? Honestly, I won't judge you—I just need to know what happened. I'm so sorry you're going this."

He struggled to make any eye contact, and appeared mesmerized by O'Brien on the outdated Magnavox Television.

"Hey man. Thanks for coming, I don't want you to get me wrong, but it's just too soon for me to talk about everything. You can't imagine how jacked up I feel right now. Look at me; all strung up like a Christmas tree. Every nurse, doctor or tech that enters this room thinks I'm a lunatic who tried to end his life," he sighed heavily.

"Dave, don't worry about them. They don't know you in the slightest. We know you, and we love you and you have to know that. Seriously, don't doubt that," I said.

"I don't usually doubt it, Turner. But something feels so vastly different in our friendship the past few months. You guys have changed," he rattled off.

"We've changed? How?" I asked, trying not to raise his blood pressure.

"You guys don't care about guy time any more. It's become 100% about chasing ass. That's not the way we were raised, and you know you shouldn't be putting yourselves in those types of situations," he scolded.

"Shit Dave! What kind of situations? I've been single for over and year. I haven't even made out with a girl lately," I laughed.

"Really?" He asked.

"Sincerely, no bullshitting. Now, Stone on the other hand," I trailed off and Dave broke a small smile.

"That aside, I need to know how I can help you, Dave. I just can't bypass that conversation. I want to know what happened. It's six in the morning, and I raced up here at light year speed because I love you. I care and I have to know what the hell is going on," I said passionately.

"Talk to me, man. I can take it. I can handle it," I said.

Pondering my thoughts, he twiddled his large thumbs.

"Fine. On one condition TJ, and I mean it," and I knew he did with every fiber of his being.

"Name it, " I retorted.

"You allow me to individually tell the others. I don't want everyone discussing this whole thing while I'm stuck up here. I can't handle the thought. It's going to take me pretty much all the courage I have to tell you," he sighed glancing at the rising sun through a small break between the curtains.

And so he began, detailing his extreme distortion from reality—ghosts and demons collecting no dust above his head because they were active plaguing his every day existence. It was so depressing. He told me he'd never found true comfort in the body of a female because they'd found no comfort in his. It all came back to Abby, the only person he'd ever loved. She had relegated him to bullshit text messages and other such jargon because her heart found happiness elsewhere. She'd fallen in love with some Michigan State law grad that was now a lawyer at a top firm in Detroit. Watching her fairytale play out from a far, as bright opportunities of his own fell through, Dave's pain amplified. How could I ignore it? How could I miss it? Just as Dave could not stop loving her, she couldn't stop from loving that other guy. What a cyclical, phenomenally depleting thing love can be.

"You're still searching and that's more than alright. So what? Maybe you're not there yet, it can take years and tears and experiences we cannot contrive to find out where we are *really* supposed to be going," I smiled back trying to convey hope.

108

Something in his head clicked; even thought it was probably temporary.

And all at once, it occurred to me that loss was entirely universal. It affected people in extraordinarily different ways. But at its core, loss isn't so different after all. I had lost Jez; Alec had lost Callie; Dave had lost Abby. All for vastly different reasons, with varying degrees of time invested. Still, it hurt each of us like hell. Pain is pain through and through.

"It'll find you, too, Turner. I know how you worry about being alone," Dave said out of the blue.

Not in the mood to argue, and passively agreeing, I replied.

"I guess I do worry about it. I hate to admit it, but I deserve love just like I believe we all do," I said.

"You risk losing everything for it, but it's worth it. You can gain infinitely in an instance. What is better than that?" He smiled for the first time all night.

"So yeah, you've been hurt. Don't forget to be willing to take the dive again. Next time could be the perfect time," I said.

"You never know. I hope *the* next girl is the girl," he said, his eyes growing heavy.

"I'm not psychic, but I have an extremely good feeling the next girl will be, Dave. You get some sleep. I'll come back and see you tomorrow," I said.

"Thanks, Turner. I'm glad it's you who came back. I needed those words. I just did. Night," Dave said yawning.

"Goodnight Dave," I said, exiting the hospital with a heart lost somewhere between happy and hazy.

Inside I wondered if we were all just one broken relationship away from a hospital bed. Was I still in puzzle pieces, broken like a child lost far from home at night, scared and confused, because of losing my own loves? Was Stone more unstable and drunk each day because of Callie? Does unrequited love have to haunt us forever?

"Run, run as fast as you can, Turner Jacobs. Push toward new things. Taste the seashore at the sea. Don't let your dreams be distant," echoed the monologue of my mother in my head. It would be insulting not to follow her wishes. She had never led me down the wrong path before. Believe deeply for love, I told myself. Believe even when that means night after night being filled with hopeful expectation that someone beautiful on the exterior and interior alike will fall in love and share a lifetime love with you. All too often it feels as if nothing good can be real. Everything bad is amplified times a million. And though I thought I would not succumb to such disastrous patterns of thought, it's inevitable after awhile for most. Just ask Dave Hector. Would Alec or I be any different? I prayed that God himself would steal the morsels of doubt away and bring me back to life—back to love.

As I cast my last thought about Dave swimming in the sea, I thought of the sea created between the universe and me, and medication came in the form of cheap, disgusting beer. Though I was channeling Stone much more than myself, I wanted to drink myself to sleep under jumping July stars and to curl my toes with sandy specks of fragmented rocks. Peace at last. Sleep was close. Goodnight and goodbye, I said aloud to the soft, pilled sheets of warm sand. Goodnight.

Across Cobbled Alleys

Chapter 9

Though I believed it to be a dream, I woke up happy in the sticky sand. Had I really slept the whole night away next to the seashore? The sun was rising over the bluebird ocean, and no normal human could stop smiling when the sun met his eye line too bright to avoid squinting.

I walked across the empty alley back to our water's edge abode. I couldn't believe my own eyes, probably still impaired from the burning of the sun and brew.

Ahead of me, in the flesh was the slender, floppy haired outline of one of my best friends in the world. Standing all of 5'9 and 130 pounds was my old pal Patrick Golfton. Patrick and I had gone to middle school together and became quite close despite our contrasting personalities. He was a quirky, introspective person who believed in the golden rule more than in Jesus. These sentiments were not popular among those in Rochester, a very religious suburb, but I always loved Patrick because he lived so kindly. He lived like Christ in many ways. At times, he was an introverted computer expert and at others, he was a rowdy extroverted soul who could make just about anyone feel at home. I always tried to see him for who I knew he was: a searching, intelligent young man who thought about things too much and not enough all at the same time. Just the sight of him, his shaggy hair and quarter size coffee brown goatee on his chin, pushed me into a landslide of memories. How strange, in an instant we can be taken back years, almost like transporting to another life or another time. Just by a particular person, sight or smell of our past.

Patrick and I often shared our deepest and most personal thoughts sitting cross-legged around a campfire or on vacation at the ocean or around a living room. It didn't matter much the location. We always found our way to the bottom of it.

"Big T! What's up, man?" He said casually, as if he had just seen me days before.

"Patrick! Shouldn't I be asking you the same question? What are you doing here and how did you find me?" I shot back with glee.

"Well I was hoping for it to be a suuuprise, but I figured ole Hector would sandbag it and tell you all, so here I am. I was talking to Dave the other day and he told me he was coming down and invited me to join. I couldn't because of work, but lo and behold work sent me to Jacksonville this week," he always emphasized words like surprise and alright and filled them with grandeur.

" That's freaking awesome, Patrick! You're still traveling a lot for work? Do you like your new job? I'm so pumped you're here. What brings you to town other than my extreme good looks?" I asked, jokingly.

"Oh you know, nothing. Work is just work. I like traveling, and my newest large account is in Jacksonville and I thought why not drive over for a weekend and see you guys while I am at it," he laughed heartily.

"You picked quite a weekend to come over. Did Dave say anything to you? He's been struggling with life really terribly lately. He's in the hospital. We think that he attempted to end it all, but no one is positively sure yet," I replied.

"He didn't say a thing. Wait, what? Ole Dave is in the hospital?" Patrick seemed shocked.

"Yeah, we don't really know what happened. He was sort of down about life, not wanting to participate in anything too much lately, but we had no idea things were so dark. If I only knew I would've changed the way I was acting around him," I shrugged my shoulders.

"I feel a messed up sense of guilt," I added.

"Knowing you, I'm sure you did what you could. That's really too bad that he felt that way. Should I go visit him? He's okay, now?" Patrick said.

Patrick and Dave were not as close as the rest of us, more acquaintances who knew one another through our group. Still, their love of all things tech gave them a common bond.

"He's doing okay, yeah. Probably no need to go visit. He's going to be released tomorrow and will probably be heading back home I'm guessing. I wouldn't worry about it," I said.

114

"Alright TJ, if you say so," Patrick replied energetically.

We sat in the dimly lit living room, opened up the windows to allow the fresh scent of saltwater into the room, and talked with the others for hours. Discussing the past, Patrick brought up the 2 A.M. drives he and I would take, wasting fuel for the sole purpose of being out and about. We never got into trouble really, we merely conversed and drove and watched the stoplights change and visited places of pertinence throughout our youthful minds. One such night, we sat on the playground at his elementary school and he sobbed. I don't remember why. Just that it created and substantiated my brotherly love for him. Men in America always seem to think some sort of catastrophe must befall them for tears to strike their cheeks, but in actuality, it's impossible not to learn that sometimes life just kicks you when you're already bloodied and on the ground. Just cry. Many nights we watched the light bend around the outline of the school we attended together, and the beacon of a full moon illuminated the surrounding skies. We were already curious, already searching—even as 16-year-old kids. We had stable homes, with loving parents and no financial obligations to cloud our visions. I nearly cried as he talked of the memories that were a distant portion of our lives—and longed for the sweetest taste of such folly and innocence.

Patrick and I understood one another from the very start of our friendship. We even shared a girlfriend in the 7th grade, much to my chagrin. With his devilish charm and prolific sense of humor, he got her to break up with me in hopes he would get her back. We laughed and sipped average coffee and delightful donuts. Stone left early to attend to a personal matter, which ultimately meant he had to try to continue to hash things out with Chelsea, and Patrick desired a nap before our night's activities. We had no extra rooms, so I showed him to mine and I proceeded to walk to the beach to pray for Dave Hector, while the others rested before dinner. "Almighty God, please bring peace. You are peace. You are comfort. You are love. You are strength," I pleaded, repeatedly until it felt like God and I were in full agreement.

***

"So other than this awful thing with Dave, what all has been going on? Anybody finding fun with the ladies of Beachside?" Patrick asked Stone and I over dinner.

"Alec is pretty involved, you could say," I laughed, nudging his ribs.

"Involved, shit. That's not really the word. I have been investing myself with a few young ladies," Stone replied satirically.

"Investing, how?" Patrick asked, clearly amused.

"Well there was Dave's cousin Blythe, and now there's this girl Chelsea, the one you met earlier at the beach house. It's all been

116

a riot really. It's also been a little bit complicated, but what great things aren't a little bit complicated? Right, Jacobs?"

"Yes, it's been a great time," I added sarcastically.

"I can't believe you hooked up with Dave's cousin. I may or may not have scanned through her pictures online before. She's looking mighty fine," Patrick smirked.

"You should see her naked," Stone added and they laughed jovially.

"Son of a gun! Jacobs, Stone is really showing you up down here. So far, I see a scoreboard of 2 to 0," Patrick joked.

"I'm taking my time, man. Really waiting for the right opportunity, but there's this new girl, Mary Kate; she's intriguing me lately. Pretty sure it's not going to go further, but who knows?" I said sheepishly.

"Well, you sound like the picture of confidence," he laughed. "Has it gone anywhere yet? I want to meet this Mary Kate. See what she's all about."

"She's awesome, but nowhere near as good looking or funny as Chelsea. Only kidding, she's a great girl," Stone smiled.

"Forget you, Stone! She's twice as sexy as Chelsea could ever be," I jabbed.

"One day, Jacobs, one day," he smiled and we ate and laughed heartily until it was time to head back to the house.

I thought heavily on our conversation as we meandered home. I was sauntering slowly and taking in the air with eyelids tightly squeezed shut. Almost hoping that if I shut down one of my five senses, that it would cause the other four senses to make exponential gains and to reach unforeseen nirvanas. Beach air, beach air, beach air. Effervescent swallows ran circles in and around my nostrils. I stared at the cross around my neck, and prayed to Jesus for any sign of strength for Dave. For Desi. For myself. I was raised to know Jesus as the ultimate vindicator— even when skeptics tried to steal my faith or convince me otherwise, I held on tightly to the promise in Christ. And don't you know, He always answers back? We're often simply far too impatient to wait for it. This time, it had to be different. As I thought of the love I had in the vestiges of my soul for Desi, Alec, and Dave—even Patrick—this time I had to wait with composure for Him. It had to be real. It wasn't worth finding love if it wasn't entirely, unequivocally, undeniably, authentic. For all of us, I prayed *that* kind of love, which could heal Dave's mind, Desi and Stone's shattered hearts, and my demoralized sense of hope, and make each of us entirely whole again.

Across Cobbled Alleys

Chapter 10

The following day upon waking, my spirit caught itself mourning in the morning—the sweet cinnamon-roll scent of the road beckoned me back to the streets of Middle America. I was homesick for the first time since we left Michigan. This particular day, my thoughts were of my Father. "If you can only be one thing, be adventurous; you can only live one life, so don't leave your questions unanswered. You get one crack at doing this thing called life correctly. The beauty is living it correctly can mean very different things to different people." He always said things like this to me as a child in the waning moonlit yellow of my childhood bedroom. As a young man with infinite possibilities at my fingertips, it was the least I could do to comply with such simple advice. Not that there was much of a choice. The desire to give all of me was buried deep within the blood vessels beneath my chalky skin. It can be the most anxiety inducing, but being born with a train of thoughts chugging along madly in my mind, who was going to stop me except myself?

Patrick knocked loudly and burst into my room before I could respond.

"Well, it's been real, Turner. Thanks for letting me hang out with you guys for the weekend."

He was always trite with his goodbyes, fearful of exposing too many of the feelings that he kept tucked comfortably inside. "Thanks for coming by. I'm glad you could make it. Safe travels back home."

"Keep me posted on Dave. I'm just a text message away," he said. I cracked a sliver of a smile and he closed the door behind himself with a half moon smile and the lift of his left hand. Suddenly, he turned and stood in the doorway and looked me square in the eyes.

"You know you can home anytime, right? You don't need to prove anything to anyone," he was abnormally serious.

"Why do you say that?" I asked him.

"I don't know. I just feel like saying it. My gut told me you needed to hear it from someone who wasn't different—someone who isn't on this adventure with you. A third party so to speak. I don't want to see you sticking it out unnecessarily. You always have a place, man. Never forget that," and with that he nodded and was off.

Minutes passed, they felt like mere seconds though, and another knock on the door. This time, it was soft and gentle. Chelsea came to the side door, which was seldom used but always open to the possibility, and entered my room carrying a smile and two Texas sized duffle bags.

"Morning Turner! How'd you sleep?" She beamed.

120

"Slept well, never enough though. How're you Chels?" and we met for a guilt hug, done out of obligation for another, rather than sheer affection.

"What's with the bag, Chels?" I asked her miffed.

"What do you mean? You know what the bags are for," she laughed.

"You're right, we're going somewhere," I played along, having no clue what she meant.

"Heck yes we are! I'm so excited to show y'all how it's done in Dallas, Texas. Y'all will absolutely love Texas. Everyone does!" She smiled brilliantly.

I didn't remember, or had forgotten, about any trip we might have planned the night before. For Patrick's last night in town, we drank three times too much, and stayed out far too late. Looking into her face, I didn't have it in my soul to disappoint her. My pupils got lost in her smile, her teeth were ivory and enormous and it was nearly impossible to see anything else on her face except those pearly whites. My homesickness dissipated for the chance of pure, unplanned adventure. Impromptu excursions were everything meaningful to me.

"I can't wait. I don't think any of us have ever been to Texas. I never have. I think after all the chaos of the last few days everyone is ready to explore somewhere new. Two weeks here has been plenty," I added. Alec is probably still sleeping. Why

don't you wake him?" I announced with a hand pointed to the
stairs.

"Oh gladly! I can't believe y'all have never been to Texas. Once
you see it, you'll never want to visit anywhere else. I'm sure he
already told you, but if he didn't, Alec told me Dave is probably
heading home to Michigan today. That's sad, but being with his
family will be the best thing God could give him," she said,
rushing upstairs to wake him. You could hear her smile even if
you couldn't see it.

Alec was typically a morning person. He was still sound asleep at
eleven, which likely indicated he was hung-over from the
previous nights outing.

A light bulb lit up in my brain. Shit! What about Callie's wedding?
So lost in our own disasters and adventures, had we lost track of
the purpose? That is the thing about a true explorers journey—
there is no clear end. It can become so convoluted. You can
proclaim an end all you want, but you won't know it until you
find it and in that very moment, the journey comes to a sense of
divine closure.

Despite the fact we were leaving seven days early, the
masses of the group were more than ready to embark on a new
journey, and to share an altogether new destination. Dave's
heartbreaking situation certainly soured the Florida mood. It
wasn't his fault—there was no resentment toward him
whatsoever—but it tainted the laidback feel the coast provided

and made all the struggles of home come to life 1,000 miles from it. It made all the bad things that existed everywhere in a fallen world explicitly clear.

Meanwhile, Desi picked Dave up from the hospital. His last evaluation went well enough for him to be signed out. His older sister drove 975 miles to pick him up, not wanting to conquer her fear of flying. Needless to say, they were products of the same environment, cut from the same cloth without a doubt.

Avoiding interaction with Dave like the plague, all members of the house found themselves abnormally busy that particular Thursday. It wasn't sure to be pretty; no one had the right words to speak. Projects around the house not previously discovered became priority number one overnight. It wasn't that we didn't want to say goodbye to Dave; no one, even the always-verbose Stone, had anything fitting, meaningful or enlightening to offer. Situations like this are the truest test of ones character. We all talk so often about helping people and blessing the world, but it's mostly clutter. What do you say to a friend who isn't much of your friend any longer and who has suffered and endured a trial this enormous? I wanted to love him with the spirit of Christ but didn't know how to do so yet. Only Desi, the person least close to Dave, could provide a fitting response to the conundrum. Ever strong in her spirit, she pulled Dave aside from the group.

"I know you have to go home now, and that is probably what's best for you, but don't lose sight of what an awesome person you are, Dave. I know it has been one terrible, horrible week, but it's just one week. You're still a funny, outgoing guy, and a great friend to everyone here. God is sure to give you peace if you ask Him for it," she spoke emphatically, trying to keep Dave's pride intact. She had words within her that grown men couldn't muster. Even if it was a matter of life and death, she stood tall in times of great peril.

"Well thanks Desi. It has been pretty awful this week, but I'm going to try to see it the way you do. Thanks for saying all that. Keep Alec and Turner in line. You never know what misadventure they might find," Dave stated.

"Right? I'll do my absolute best," she said, hugging Dave goodbye uncomfortably.

"Well, we better go now. The road to Michigan doesn't get any shorter standing around here. See you around guys," Dave said.

"Safe trip home, Dave." the group replied in near perfect unison.

The house looked sad as we drove away. As if homes contained emotions, I could see it crying— a sweet spring rain from it's windows and dew dripping from it's gutters. Looking back, telling the sweet house not to fret, maybe one day we'd be back again. Would it be for the wedding next week or years later? None of us were completely sure when it'd be. Attending that wedding began to feel as much like my purpose as exploration. Convincing Alec and Desi of the same might be a stretch, but if anyone could do it, why not me?

I looked back at Dave and his sister. They packed her Honda and both braced for their time on the road. So outré, two vehicles, two destinations, two directions, six people, tied in a flip-flop spider web spiral and yet, walking very much alone on their own. It was twisted, strange and messy, but it was beautiful to see so many wide-eyed people searching simultaneously. Dave's departure was more than a simple writer can put into prose; it was, and as I got older I understood this so much more clearly, just another of many, many distorted turns in this life— and just one of the many goodbyes I'd have to endure. I hadn't gotten use to practicing my somber, stiff face that I wore as Dave left. The overwhelming feeling that it'd be forever long until I saw Dave Hector again stole any chance of a smile away from me. If this was the end of our friendship, I was thankful for each moment and memory we had together. You can't look back asking what if or what could have been. Because I believe wholeheartedly that the past has an unusual way of creating tracks in the snow to follow for a better future. I would be a fool to believe anything less.

***

Chelsea, who was frenzied and excitable for Alec, interrupted my daydreaming. I could see their chemistry finally, touching slowly, giggling until their eyes rolled back into their heads. Tears nearly coming down their blush red cheeks. I couldn't help but be thrilled... and jealous. Chelsea nodded off to sleep eventually, Desi did too, and Stone drove and looked over at me and whispered words softly so as to not wake the sleeping beauties in our car.

"Turner, it all makes sense. I understand this life, the whole damned purpose, but when it comes down to it, the entire living part doesn't make me any happier."

"What do you mean? You seem pretty happy lately. I've been feeling like you've turned a corner since Blythe left and things with Chelsea took off," I said.

"Maybe I have. It's bizarre right? Our purpose, yes we see it, and perhaps we can truly find it, but happiness exists outside of purpose sometimes. I know happiness is partly a choice. I hate to say it but I've been thinking that maybe, just maybe, we're all one-step away from being the person who runs away from everything forever. Some would call that an adventurer, others a mad man. Don't you ever worry that'll happen to you? Maybe, just maybe you'll cross the line from free spirited adventurer to mad man?" He asked, pensively.

I admired his pensive side. It provoked such great thought in me, as well.

126

"I think I want to believe that those people who are broken hearted, like our buddy Dave Hector, are so far gone compared to what we could possibly be, even at our worst, but maybe we're closer to that after all. Perhaps we've just learned how to mask the pain better. It's our courage, masking how bad and messy and hauntingly awful some things actually are," my heart ached as I responded.

I continued, "Yeah, some days you'd think I'm scraping myself from the clay...we've been groomed to mask our burdens. That's why it's instrumental, Alec, absolutely critical in fact, that we have people like each other who get it too, so we don't end up loosing every last fragment of sanity and going trippy insane in our brains. Sometimes we have to talk about the way we feel," I stated with confidence.

He laughed, but it wasn't humorous. Clearly lost in another world, another train of thought, he spoke up.

"Fuck Geraldo," raising his voice from a whisper.

"What? What are you talking about?" I laughed loudly, not catching the out of left field reference.

"No, listen. Remember my cousin Geraldo?"

"Yeah, I remember you mentioning him before but," he cut me off.

"Forget that bastard. I remember as a kid at my Grandma's house, my cousins would all stay up there together for a week or so in the summer. It was a rural place, somewhere in

Washington. There wasn't much to do but tell stories and play games around the property. We laughed a lot during the day. I liked almost all of my cousins, with the exception of one: Geraldo. I tried to like him, I swear, but he was slow. I can remember every last detail about how annoying spending time with him was. I can hear every horrific sound from his pubescent voice, the attempted stubble on his face, the way he pushed his glasses up with his forefinger. I fucking hated him. He drove me insane. Well, anyway, here I was, in this bed that makes crinkling noises because it has a liner on it because Geraldo pisses the bed. And yeah, I know I'm not altogether perfect, I can even acknowledge lately I am struggling, but living life can be like having to put up with my drug addicted, compulsive liar of a cousin Geraldo," he said exasperated.

His eyes were glaring with anger and I could see him hot air balloon high. I didn't know how to talk him down, so as only a great friend can, I joined in. Our camaraderie was often in our dialogue but on this given night our friendship sat draped in non-vocalized terms.

A far off tree strayed and each branch distracted me to a different vein of consciousness, of life, and Stone began to sigh heavily, and I placed my hand on his sunken shoulder.

"We'll chase, chase, chase but all for naught? We're just ants but we think we're satellites you know it? We think we're the moon and the stars and then we meet someone we suppose could actually be our moon and our stars like Callie. And as they burn out, ultimately, so do we. But Stone—though this is an enormous *but*—every dog has his day. And you'll have yours. And I'll have mine. If not for a million years of suffering, our day will indeed come," I said.

"Life doesn't have to be like a week with Geraldo," I ended.

It didn't stop his slow, withdrawn weep murmuring on, but I know it stung him at his caring core. I wondered if today might be Stone's day. Or week. Or month. Or year. Or if this was just another whimsically transposed star awaiting its chance to shut out the light forevermore. Glancing off at Chelsea, I thought better of his chances than my own. It seemed like she might be around awhile. Was this mini breakdown the start of his next chapter? I hoped so with all my heart. It is not uncommon to breakdown before the blindingly beautiful daylight breaks in.

"She's better than I deserve. I'm not even sure why she wants me," he said.

"Because you're a great guy. And Chelsea is the kind of girl who can see through the vibrato. She can look right down to your heart and know what you're all about," I replied.

"That's what I'm afraid of," he contended.

"Rightfully so. You're a real numb nuts sometimes," I uttered back.

"Thanks asshole. I'm going to do my best to keep her around," he insisted.

And I believed him.

As Stone's day came upon us, or so it felt, I could only ponder: was my day also near? I always talked to fill in the silence, because that's the way I'm wired, I'm the happy go lucky optimist living buried internally in pessimism and defeat, and telling jokes to make it all work. But does it ever work? Girls enter and they exit. Dollars and stories—heartfelt testimonies of pitiful pains and wonderful recreation and memories accumulated over a lifetime— hearts were exchanged too easily. Does anything ever come of it in the inner most fragment of our soul? Am I entirely too complacent and impatient to wait around for anything beautiful and bizarre to begin?

I wanted to be in love, more than ever in my life. I ached for love. Doesn't every single human being ache for it with all their might at some point in their life? Why do I think I am any different? I guess because my whole life the entire world has told me love exists and it is out there for me to snatch up, when the time comes. Yet, here I am, still eclectically wandering about the US of A looking for something I don't *positively* know that I will find. Something that I don't know exists, really. Maybe next month or next year the right person will enter and if it doesn't and all hope is lost and transformed into a shot of liqueur tossed down the throat—quickly consumed and forever gone. I promised myself I would find my own way to make those around me silly smile. I would not conform to the world and its mounting guilty pleasures. And wouldn't you know it, I wouldn't have to. My smile would be coming to stay before too long.

Across Cobbled Alleys

Chapter 11

More roads traveled, and my sister was still cast off to sleep wrapped like some mummy in the queen sized pink blanket.

"I have to have it!" she exclaimed upon seeing it. Almost nothing in the world made me happier than when my younger sister conjured up a smile. I had to buy it for her on the spot.

With freckled face nose twitching, pink iPhone headphones blaring instrumental music, she existed in a stratospheric peace that we all long to taste. Desi had a way of shoving all that stressed her out to the back burner and continually found new and beautiful ways to thrive-live-breathe-and enjoy her life. There was no method to the madness; she existed happily because her concerns did not concern her. It was a double-edged sword of course, her priorities could get easily jumbled within her abundant lack of concern, but often she found her way. I envied it about her. If only I could simply dust off my fears. I knew her fears still found her in weakened states, but not like mine, not like Stone's. It was like comparing the swimming pool in the backyard of our childhood home to the Pacific Ocean.

The vent was pushing cool air onto my knees so alarmingly freezing that I longed for the sweet sweat of the

132

outdoors. I was deep in thought, all too often an occurrence, thinking of the previous years. It was Father's Day and I missed my dad. Every time I drove, my mind took a long-winded journey with me. Often reflecting on my past, my youth, world issues and problems, my loved ones—essentially, everything known to a twenty something American man.

A memory I couldn't forget was spending Fathers Day 2012 playing "Father" to two young African American boys that lived next door. Knowing that the boys' actual Father's happened to be visibly absent, Desi suggested we let them tag along on most of our endeavors. I realized that they loved me and didn't care about who I was. They cared simply that I was willing to spend time with them. The root of love is quality time, however you define it. The boys defined quality time as running around the beach throwing the football or swimming or playing video games, all the while being boisterous as firecrackers.

Davon, an athletically built eleven-year-old toned in muscle mass nearly as much as I, had landed in American a year prior from Jamaica. His skinny ten-year-old cousin Tyus, who was better known as "Little Man," lived with Davon and his mother. Through spending days and afternoons with Davon and Little Man, it became clear to me that being a parent is a 24/7 profession, yielding little appreciation in the present. For all the uncomfortable silences that we shared—it could be that way with anyone though—there were innumerable things learned by all of us. Probably during this time, I learned the most about life.

As the boys jumped, 360-ed, frolicked and fell amongst the navy blue tipped waves of the Lake Michigan, they displayed a genuine zest— happiness on speed dial that I could no longer channel. Oh, to be ten again, riding my bike, desirous of only summer and sun and superman ice cream. Their foray into the waves, unbridled spirits and willingness to let go of every unfair thing in their lives—that alone taught me to persevere. Maybe that's part of the whole deal—you get taught by those you think you're teaching. And in the end, both people leave the relationship stronger and better prepared to confront the challenges that will surely come later. Tyus spun and spun, and continually fell face first into the water like he had never seen it before. The best part about the whole thing was that he didn't even mind the salt water burning his eyes red. It's that type of freedom we all desire. Carelessness becomes less present with age until every choice we make is so calculated we know what we'll decide long before we have the opportunity to determine it. What's the fun in knowing the ending of our story while it's still unfolding?

***

Alec Stone broke the silence of my daydream.

"Jacobs, do you remember that girl Ellie from our vacation a few years back?" Did I ever.

"Pretty impossible to forget, wouldn't you agree?"

We both chuckled in unison.

"I wonder what ever happened to her. That night I met her, holy shit, I thought I was going to marry her. She was as feisty a girl as I've ever met. I love a little feistiness in my gals, ya' know? I can't believe we had to go 1,000 miles away to meet people who lived 30 miles away from home," he remarked.

"You aren't telling me anything I don't know. I still can't believe Callie never found out that you hooked up with Ellie. To think that Callie and Ellie even had mutual friends back home, you are a sneaky son of a bitch," I snorted.

"I have my moments, Jacobs. All I remember clearly from that night was when your eyes were rolling in the back of your head because you were altogether smashed and you invited her and her friends over to grab a drink. That was not your worst decision of all time," he smiled.

"You're only saying that because you got laid Alec—"

He looked at Chelsea and darted his eyes back to me.

"Jacobs, watch what you're saying man! It wasn't about all of that," Stone murmured passively.

It didn't matter what we said or how loud we said it. Chelsea had her iPhone headphones on and was sleeping with her mouth dripping and drooling onto the seatbelt.

"All I remember, Alec, is that you said she was the best you'd ever had," I whispered.

"That she was Jacobs, that she was…" He looked off into the distance as if he was reminiscing about the drunken encounter that could only have been described as egregiously sloppy.

"Who knows any more? That was a long time ago. I definitely wouldn't mind the chance to see her naked once again," he laughed evilly.

I shot him a *what the hell* look, especially after he had just told me to pipe down with my comments about his past with Chelsea around.

"I think it would best serve you to live in the here and now. No time like the present to chase away your frustration. We're really living right now; do you feel it? In this blessed and exact moment as we transverse this country, we are *truly* living. And you, have a hell of a chance to keep the dream alive," I said, pointing at the beautiful girl behind his seat.

"No need to lecture me, I know I have the world by it's strings," Stone said, visibly excited.

As we crossed into the largest state in America, I smiled at the thought of my former dream and her incredible ability to make me relax with goofy faces and bathroom humor. Her beauty was negated all too often by her overwhelming sense of brokenness. Something the size of Texas hit me as we entered the state; maybe every positive relational encounter was about someone leaving the relationship better off than when they entered. It didn't matter if the "encounter" was a conversation that happened only one time or a love affair that lasted for years. You have to let your mind decide to be free of worry and to press onward looking for something positive to take away from every person who ever touches your life.

In my quest to obtain genuine and true love, I couldn't keep my eyes shut any longer. I smiled and waited because sometimes that is all one can do. I had left everyone and everything purposeful to find happier times and invigorating encounters. I left better off each time, even if it took me months or years to see so. We all leave for varying reasons, but often, our struggle is worth its weight in growth.

***

We pulled into the affluent Dallas suburb of Highland Park around 10 p.m. on a Thursday evening with rain hitting the windshield like 1,000 dancing needles. Shaking, I awoke to find myself slick with sweat and my hair crisscrossed and matted into my pillowcase. A slender figure exited the front door, running unabashed through the stormy weather as our car pulled into the driveway.

"Chelsea! Hey sis! So glad you're home," she giggled happily.

"Laura Belle! I missed you so much," she said, faking a kissing sound as she hugged her sister sweetly.

"Everybody this is my beautiful baby sister Laura," Chelsea shrieked.

Laura looked almost nothing like her older sister. Chelsea's raven colored hair and seawater blue eyes drew your attention. She wore tight, curve grabbing clothes and showed off her natural beauty. Laura possessed a simple, but elegant frame—small eyes and slender, oval face. Her nose was too large for her face, and heavily made up to cover the pockmarked skin beneath. She had plenty of freckles under her grass green eyes. She wore a baggy Texas Longhorns long sleeve T-Shirt and sweatpants.

We were all introduced and I could tell Stone was in no such mood to powwow in the garage, taking cover from the rain showers. His weariness, which was held in small pockets in his upper cheeks, had sunk low as his chin. His evident desire to sleep was ignored by Chelsea and the girls, as they conversed merrily. He didn't utter a word.

After the girls chattered like they had been apart for several years, I yawned obnoxiously.

"I'm beat. I think I'm going to go to bed now if that's cool."

Chelsea smirked, almost agitated by my remark.

"At least you didn't have to stay up all night keeping the driver alert!" She poked Alec's gut and snickered gleefully. He didn't move a muscle, except for a small "hump" sound.

"Right, right. Our expert navigator must be tired," I said looking off at Stone who rolled his eyes softly.

"Chelsea, we really should get these boys to bed. Especially your Alec," Laura laughed playfully and turned on her heel to enter the sprawling Texas mansion. I failed to capture the magnitude of this monstrous home in suburban Dallas, most likely due to road fatigue. A lethargy that is all too familiar on the road, plaguing and tugging at the eyes. But you keep on pushing forward toward the next endeavor under God's voluminous skies. Road warriors are meant to conquer the road ahead regardless of where it leads. Sleep is for the dead.

Laura showed us to our rooms in the East Wing of the sprawling home, while Desi and Chelsea grabbed a glass of wine from the kitchen. A mass text arrived about three minutes later from Stone:

"I'm exhausted. Please let me sleep until at least 10. Goodnight." I cracked a half-smile moon; this ebb and flow was the madman at his finest. Entirely frustrated maybe, but entirely in control.

I rolled into Egyptian cotton sheets in hopes of finding peace in the Texas summertime on a bed that conveyed old money opulence and royalty. The comforter was a hand knit quilt of maroon and gold and it felt expensive and antique. I nestled in slowly, gently almost anticipating the winter like quiver given off from cool sheets and let my mind drift into rest.

Like a phantom, ragged run ghost creatures suffocated the last lapses of breathe from my weak lungs. I saw her face. Everywhere I was and went the distance I'd covered—it was irrelevant. In a mist, my soul, fragile and youthful, sometimes altogether weak, was burdened by the face of Jez once again.

Every time any new relational encounter failed around my life, with my close compatriots or myself, the penetrating pain and somber sting came back and my mind raced back to her. I couldn't understand why. Rejection tastes the most bitter from someone you once trusted completely. Her cheeky grin, sunlight streaked blonde hair, hazel eyes—they were all slowly, methodically eating me alive. I thought I'd buried these crosses? I thought traveling the country and exploring on my own would steal the bitterness and unequivocal torment from my life? Sadness knows no state lines.

Jezebel will forget me; her life will go on. I'll even forget her someday too. That much I do know with certainly. And though I didn't want to admit it, I was too weak to know that there was a better future in front of me than anything I experienced in my past. If only I could have known then what I know now. But you can't learn from simply sitting still, so I kept ambling onward chasing the word *hope* until every last bit of the past was vacuumed out of my life for good.

Across Cobbled Alleys

Chapter 12

Approaching the beach club pool at Highland's finest housing development, Woodland Dunes, I walked in solitude with headphones in. Sometimes I put them in as if to announce to the world my great desire for silence. This was one of those occasions. Often I got so immersed in the music and the created world on my insides. I could be shocked back to reality in one fell swoop. And like clockwork, my palms were sweat covered, eyes flushed and my heart rate accelerated. I couldn't believe my own four eyes. There she sat, veiled behind multicolored aviator sunglass lenses with her light brown ponytail tucked into a baseball cap.

"Ma-ma-Mary Kate? What're you doing here?" I stammered painfully.

"Hey Turner! Where's everybody? I'm here to surprise Chelsea for her birthday! Her mom and I planned for me to join all y'all secretly," she stated it so pleasantly, so casually. You would've thought we were family friends or something. There was no apparent tension in her approach. She seemed genuinely at ease, void of any strange feelings but I felt genuinely dripped in awkward sentiments. Still, I loved the way she said Chelsea. It reminded me of Tom Hanks in Forrest Gump. She actually was from a small town only an hour from the fictional town Forrest called home.

My disbelief began marinating in my bubbling blood and all I wanted to do was run away from Texas in a fleeting panic stricken moment. I hadn't even been there a day. I talked myself down realizing it wasn't that all together tense between us. We had experienced nothing worth creating tension over. Sometimes my immature twenty two year old self saw things through grief stained lenses. My greatest weakness was always the same; experiencing rejection at the hands of the opposite sex.

Looking desperately for someone to save me from entertaining another one of Alec's lovers' female friends, our footsteps felt frozen like we were marching in molasses toward the mansion. Chelsea was in the kitchen talking with her Mother about her birthday plans and the new guy she had been romancing, Alec Stone. Desi roamed the back porch and Alec was incoherent and sound asleep. So, there we sat, two former flames burnt out with breakneck speed, making conversation about the others and the weather and the altogether evident. Nothing about our conversation was concrete; it was muddled and messy, and the dialogue between us was mostly bullshit tossed into the sober atmosphere. I longed to be saved by the others more than ever before. Someone save me so I can wander back to the pool to submerge my thoughts in music.

Finally, I grabbed her a drink and chugged one myself.

142

I interrupted the pleasantries and became direct.

"Why didn't you ever call me back? I had a lot of fun on our date. It seemed like you did too. I just didn't get why you never got back to me after such an awesome evening," I asked.

"Our date was so much fun, seriously it was, but I knew that we couldn't work out, that's why I never called back. You live in Michigan. I'm in college for two more years at Auburn. What's the point of us parading around as something we're not?" She asked.

"Yeah, I get what you're saying. I just wanted another chance to prove to you there could be something special between us. You basically shut the door before I could knock again," I remarked.

"I'm sorry. I didn't hurt you, did I? I didn't intend to or anything. I just thought it for the best we create some distance before one of us got in too deep too soon," she stated, clearly referencing how giddy I had been on our date.

"No, I'm not hurt," I lied. "You're probably right. The distance would have been impossible. I overreacted big time. Can you forgive me?" I asked politely. I was so desperate for peace; I would have done anything to bridge the gap between her and I.

"You have nothing to apologize for. You're an amazing guy and some girl is going to be so lucky someday," she batted her eyelashes.

"Same to you MK. You already know it, but you're an amazing catch," I countered.

One by one the rest of the party trickled into the living room ready to go to the beach club. Upon arrival, all shared quizzical looks and glances, and embraced MK's presence in Dallas. Chelsea shrieked with giddy girl joy like a teenager.

"MK, my gosh, how in the world? How did you get here?" Chelsea smiled.

"I flew here, silly," Mary Kate jabbed and grinned wide as the freeway.

"Aw! Two weeks apart and you just couldn't stand to be away from me?" Chelsea played.

"Well, when you put it that way..." MK prodded.

This was the epitome of their amusing relationship; playful and restless, jabbering and jawing forever, they laughed like children until they were on their knees. You couldn't help but love seeing their unbridled jubilation.

As the sun baked our skin like vegetables, we looked at the meadows surrounding the fenced in pool and the girls frolicked about in the clear-blue water with glee. Stone and I stretched across two patio pool chairs, made of gently finished blonde wood. Stone nudged the chairs to the edge of the water, and I followed. He pulled his earphones loose from the older-than-Adam iPod his parents gave him for our high school graduation. He didn't say much, but in it, he said everything.

"This is sure going to be interesting. I mean if we stay here long enough to figure this all out," he said.

144

"What do you mean?" I replied.

"Well you know me, Chelsea is exciting. She's bright eyed and her breasts, well, they speak for themselves, but who knows? I can't just set up shop here with her. This is a fling, Turner," he said as if I could read his thoughts.

It was an iconic Alec response, laden with crassness and deep pontification, simultaneously attempting to coexist.

"We need to go back to Florida pretty soon, Alec. We need to get to the wedding. We have a week to figure this shit out. I understand that you have an adventure to dig into here, and it's cool. It gives me time to clear my head. At this point, that's the best present anyone could ever give me," I grimaced.

"You make a valid point, my friend. But so what about the wedding? It's still a week away. Plenty of time to figure that shit out. Do we go? Do I ignore it and just dig in with this Chelsea girl? Do I abandon both situations altogether? Is that what you're implying?"

Of course I was implying the opposite quite clearly. I scoffed, laughing at his nonsensical comments.

He spoke casually, almost as if he hardly knew Chelsea. In hindsight, I suppose that they didn't really know one another all that well. Chelsea was the piece that picked up where Blythe left off.

145

"We need to at the least try to go, don't you think? Wasn't that part of the point of this whole trip? For you to feel vindicated or ridden of Callie at long last?" I posed.

"Turner, that wasn't entirely the point of leaving. Did you really think it was only about Callie? No, it was about getting the hell out of Michigan and finding something else—anything else—that makes sense. You know finding something bigger than me and my past and my life and yours, too. Tell me you see that? Tell me that's clear to you?"

"Of course I can see that, Alec. I wouldn't be here, still on this journey if I didn't see it. I just don't want you to regret missing the chance to show up at her wedding and seeing the look on her face..." we smiled and laughed but Stone's was so half-hearted. It seemed like he was throwing in the towel on going without saying a word, subtly backing his way out of this like he had from other challenges too many times before.

"Be patient, Turner. I'll figure all of this out soon and so will you. Don't worry about it all though, you can't get lost in your thoughts," he turned and made himself comfortable with eyes closed.

"Easy for you to say. We're going to go. I want to see you through this whole ordeal man. Speaking of unique situations, I have to ask you...what do I do in regard to this whole Mary Kate scenario? Anything? Or should I leave it be?"

The aforementioned female, twenty-five feet away, was bobbing in and out of the enormous pool like a fishing lure, smiling each time she came above the surface.

"What's there to talk about? Nothing happened with her. It didn't go anywhere. No mess to clean up, the way that I see it. You liked her far too much; she didn't like you quite as much. Open and shut case," he stated matter of fact.

"I know, but she still makes me feel anxious. I see her mile wide smile and I melt a little bit, even though I really shouldn't be feeling so jittery around her," I replied.

"Why? You had two dates! It truly isn't worth having anxiety about. Look at her like a family friend or something. Just relax," Stone said, pacifistically.

The truth he spoke hurt, but it was accurate. Sweet loneliness, having no woman in my life, had made me more awkward than I had ever been.

"It's simple. You are going to find someone who makes your heart beat—your heart tick right out of your chest so fast it can't slow down. This clearly isn't that girl. However, I do know a girl that might suit your fancy who will likely be at the wedding, if we go. She's a friend of Callie's younger sister, the hot one. Can you guess whom I'm thinking of?" he smiled.

He always talked with a tilt of his head—primarily to the right—and often expressed feeling and emotions with his hands—bitten fingernails and all.

"Let me guess. Anna Bishop?"

"Yeah, so you remember her?" Alec asked.

"Couldn't possibly forget a girl with a body like that. I don't know her well or anything, but I've met her. Sometimes she texts me," I said.

"She's a beauty, right?" He quipped happily

"Downright stunning. She's kind of young though, isn't she? She has to be like 18, right?" I asked.

"Yeah, something like that. Don't concern yourself with the details. Just let it happen," he nodded excessively.

"After the MK debacle, I'm not sure if I can just let anything happen. I don't know if it's a good idea man. Am I really ready?" I asked rhetorically because I knew I was ready. I was just scared after being out of the game for too long and failing on my first attempt back in it.

"No room for that kind of negativity, Turner. MK is an anomaly, nothing more. She's a figment of your imagination that caught your attention when you were weak. Forget about her. I'm telling you I will reintroduce you to Anna if we see her there. What do you have to lose? Honestly?" he rolled his eyes behind a pair of sunglasses that he stole from me.

"Not very much," I responded, almost too eagerly.

"It's settled then. You have five days to prepare yourself Turner Jacobs. Prepare well, grasshopper. She's a firecracker and a half from what I hear," he said jokingly.

"So are you saying that we're going to the wedding?" I asked excitedly.

"No guarantees, but if it will get you back in the game, what kind of friend would I be if I said no?"

"I'll be ready," I replied and smiled. I buckled my hypothetical seatbelt for what could be another bumpy ride. I'd seen stranger tides, in far off lands, and had felt far more mystified and disillusioned than this simple form of such feelings today.

Before I knew it, my brain synapses fired uncharted back to those places—feelings of confidence and success. I once had it. I could remember it vividly. It was time to find it fully again. The only way to really attain it was to go, to leap, and to run full steam ahead toward my goal of getting back in the game wholeheartedly. I could sit back no more. I had been sitting back on a journey that had been one of the most enormous leaps of my life. Leaving Michigan was a gigantic first step in the right direction, but now, the clock struck metaphorical midnight and today was a new day and it was all mine to run like I knew I could all along. Next stop, Anna Bishop.

Across Cobbled Alleys

Chapter 13

I made up my mind to hate Texas and every last thing about its isolationist ideologies before I had arrived. The stench of the dry-sick air, the commercialization, and the masses of people, who bought up the commercialization so pervasively, sickened me. The thing that perturbed me most was the outwardly Christian aesthetic. There was constant professing of "Jesus" and "faith" and the cross everywhere all the time—but so few Texans I interacted with tried to live like Him. Isn't that what this whole thing is about anyway? I make a mess of things with regularity, but I'm trying to live like Him at least. Sure, failure is the epithet of the whole story, but lofty dreams and continual desire to improve kept me from succumbing to early defeat. Faith is nothing to be taken half-heartedly. Theoretically, I should have loved all the opportunities Texas provided for adventure, but no matter. To me, it was just one oversized wasteland where people spoke one way and lived another. Did I fit handsomely into this group of those who talk but can't walk? Sometimes we can fit just about anywhere, and in my worst moments, I belonged. I could camouflage myself just the same. So looking up at the speckled spacious Texas stars that shone so brightly in my eyes, I resolved to the next chapter.

The Texas heat had run me down to fumes of nothing, and the crew had embarked on a day trip to Arkansas, where Chelsea's family had a lake house. I wanted to go, I should have gone, but I felt too miserable to make it. MK, and the altogether feeling that my thoughts were mere annoyance, resulted in a nasty combination. Still, I tried to get my confidence up to see Anna Bishop at Callie's wedding.

Our relationship had been much more passive than aggressive, much more far out and unrealistic than meaningful and authentic, but God can make miracles out of molehills. For some reason, I was drawn to Anna like glue. I always told myself she was too young for me or one of another million excuses about how she liked guys who played baseball and I didn't play baseball or she was moving away for college etc., but was four years younger really that much of a difference? Was playing basketball much different than playing baseball? Was distance actually important in a long-term courtship? Or was something much more meaningful brewing on the horizon line of my life? I didn't really know her, so in the house from a far, I idealized her as perfect. I am so guilty of idealizing things I do not know as being better than the things that I have. Isn't that part of the male suffering? I prayed for patience and my ability to be thankful for what I had, all the while wondering about Anna.

Moments later, the door opened and it was Chelsea. She lingered in the doorway, swinging on the woodwork near the entrance to my room.

"I hope this isn't awkward, but I need to ask you something about Alec."

"Always. What's up?"

"Does he ever discuss his feelings with you? Like about he and I?" She asked, innocently.

My brain began racing. Here it goes again. This whole Texas thing is going to blow up to smithereens in our faces because of Stone's inability to commit to anything. Even the things and the people that were worthwhile like Chelsea.

"Occasionally he does, but you know he's not one to share his feelings openly," I said lying with a straight face. I couldn't break her heart. It wasn't mine for the breaking.

"Maybe he's just not sure about it all yet.... this is a fairly new thing," I replied hoping to save her spirit.

"I know it hasn't been very long, but it all feels so real. He is one of those next level guys that you can see yourself settling down with," she attempted to restrain the emotion in her face, but failed.

"He is something, that's true. He is the greatest friend I've ever had really. I can't say I really know the whole truth of it, but I don't know that he's ready to make a commitment. He's figuring out so many things within himself right now," I countered.

"Really? Should I talk to him about whatever he's working through?"

"Totally up to you. I could always chat with him for you?" I mentioned, as I had many times before to many other girls.

"No, no. I'm a big girl. I can handle Alec by myself just fine," she defended.

"Oh, I know that. When his feelings are involved, he can be a tough read. If you change your mind, let me know," I said.

"Seriously, thanks for listening. But I think I know just the way to handle it," she proclaimed, shutting the door behind her bodacious behind swiftly.

There was something elementary and charming about her responses. If only any beautiful female would fight so strongly for me. If anyone had in fact fought for me with such zeal and charm, I'd likely find myself a taken man... My heart locked and kept up readily for only one woman. Women always think it's only the man that must pursue; in actuality, a woman must also pursue a man's heart back with fortitude or it's all for naught really. Love was never intended to be a one-way street.

***

Storms were stirring Texas and shaking the sparse palms trees like twigs. The weather mirrored Stone. He was disillusioned and emotional as we entered Chelsea's Infiniti G35 for our first day at Wallace Pharmaceuticals in the outskirts of downtown Dallas, in a suburb named Frisco. Her Dad needed help for a few days around the office and when he asked us if we were interested in making a few bucks, we agreed to help him out. It was the least we could do for allowing us to stay in his house, to eat his food, and in Alec's case, to have his daughter.

It was a twenty-minute drive, but with all the worry and the weather, the traffic had us gridlocked going nowhere fast. Twisting his bottled water cap repeatedly, fidgeting around in the passengers seat, Stoned looked blankly out the window into the sideways rain. The skies were nearly opaque and my vision was blurred ahead of me. I didn't feel like talking much either, but was curious to his thoughts.

"So, what's going on man? You've hardly said a word today," I posed.

"It's nothing man. I'm just tired," and it was eerily cognizant of a conversation with a woman.

"Come on. You're a fool if you think that's an answer I'll believe," I said cheerily as if to appear that I was joking.

"Lots on my mind these past few days. But I don't really want to talk about it," he moaned.

"Like what? Thinking about what the hell you're going to do with this whole Chelsea situation?" I prodded.

154

"Can't you leave it be for once, man? You always pry; you always ask me so many questions about what I'm thinking. Sometimes you need to sit still," he stated, agitated.

I tried not to be offended, but deep down my insides were tender with embarrassment.

 "I'm not trying to invade your privacy or whatever, and I certainly don't mean to pry. We can just let it go, man," I replied upset.

"I'm sorry man, I'm overreacting for whatever reason, and you know it's not you—it's Chelsea and me. I'm probably more confused than I was with Blythe and I can't sleep and I feel weak; so alone and weak, even with everybody around. Am I some kind of lunatic?" He ranted.

Pandora's box had been opened with a rip roar and Stone was swimming amongst his personal flood here on the roadways of The Lone Star State.

"She is starting to wonder what's going on with the two of you, but who says you need to know all that right now? You'll figure this out like you always do," I said, hopeful.

"You think so? I'm glad you're so confident it will work itself out," Alec said with sarcasm in his speech.

"Yeah, I can't know for sure what the right answer is, but I hope it works out for both of you. We're coming to the end of this snake tongue-twisting journey. Enjoy the rest of the ride while we can, Stone. Just remember, there are only so many Chelsea's in the world," I shrugged.

"It's just not that simple for me lately. I came on this adventure to escape the hardships existing in my stagnant Michigan life—to separate myself from girls, feelings and all of those around me who are getting married and boring and lifeless overnight. So, I go on this adventure, and I am realizing every place is a variation of the same thing as at home. The same complications, same pains, same cloaked smiles; I guess I'm beginning to see that it's the same thing painted just a little differently, everywhere you go," Stone stated dramatically.

"I get what you're saying Alec, but take a step back. At least we're doing something! We're fighting the boredom and apathy that all the others are buying by the bucket load. We're actually forging a path distinctly our own. No one on this Earthly planet can touch that. The memories are ours forever," I declared passionately.

"That's an awesome thing Turner—it is. And I am absolutely glad I came here, but I'm just not sure I love the path I created thus far. I feel like it's been more trial and error, just as it always has been before," he sighed heavily, the windows near his lips clouded.

I *wanted* to tell him that there was nothing wrong with trial and error. To tell him he needed to deconstruct the negative thoughts surrounding his transgressions. To tell him that there were no definitively *correct* choices on this journey. And to tell

156

him a girl like Chelsea deserved a man who could make a decision and stick to it. There was no need to string this whole thing along much more than we already had. He began to speak before I could utter a fragment.

"I don't want to break her heart, Turner. And selfishly, I don't want mine to break either. I know she's remarkable and so beautiful, but we aren't even having sex and the appeal to do so is less for me each day because I know I can't keep her. I know she'll never be mine fully. I'm a hard person to know, but you already know that. I think I've come to terms with it this week," he said.

He wasn't altogether hard to know; he wasn't hard to befriend or to experience life with, but sincere relationships and love are a burden too taxing for a wandering heart. In spite of this, he always seemed to remain involved with someone. I never knew why, or even how—but he was always charming the pants off of someone and almost always taken.

"Her heart might break, Alec, but that's a risk you took by picking her. Everyone's heart does at one time or another. If it doesn't break because of you, it'll be someone else. We all have to know genuine heartache to in turn know the most authentic love."

"That's probably true," he sheepishly smiled.

"Plus, she has a great family, people who love her unconditionally who will help her out. This isn't like repeating the Blythe situation. This is something totally different. So don't worry about all of the comparison that might be going on in your head. I will say though, if any piece of your heart wants her, you have to stay. She's the kind of girl that may be worth all the trouble," I shot at him.

"I need to think about that," Alec replied.

"If you need to think about it, you probably already have your answer," I said.

"Maybe I do," he said.

We exited the car and both cracked cordial smiles to show understanding. We walked quickly into the office complex, out of the blowing rain, and picked up our badges at the front desk to gain access to Wallace Pharmaceuticals.

"Alec, you have until tomorrow to tell me if we are going to the wedding for sure or if you are staying in Dallas. Deal?"

"I'll try my best, but I can't make any promises that I can make a decision that quickly. Why do you have to be in such a rush?" Alec asked.

"I just want to know what's going on already. You aren't the only one affected by this whole ordeal, man," I replied, annoyed.

"You think I don't know that? Of course I know that," he said, grabbing his mop and dragging it across the floor pacifistically.

"Then act like it," I declared defiantly, eyes lit up bright like Christmas lights.

"This is far more about *your* future and *your* adventure than it is mine. This whole ordeal began because you showed up on my driveway at midnight with the need to get the hell out of Michigan and I was depressed and hopeless just enough that I decided to join you in a moment of weakness," I exclaimed.

"Turner, give me a fucking break. This is as much about your own need to fulfill the "adventurous" side you always tell people you have as it is about my need to find something bigger, grander and utterly harmonious within my soul," Alec fumed, albeit poetically.

"I don't need to prove anything. Not to you or to anyone. I know who I am dammit. And if you, my best friend of nearly 10 years cannot see that, maybe something is getting lost in translation. I left Michigan because my best friend in the whole world needed me. Yeah, I wanted to leave but I wouldn't have left it weren't for you, Alec," I shouted, fighting back tears of anger.

He sat back, clearly pondering, and bit his cuticles with his teeth. He started to clear his throat loudly and threw the final blow.

"You remember how calm I was when Dave attempted suicide, right?" He questioned. I nodded in agreement.

"That's because I'd been feeling the same way. I thought about killing myself a few times. I began to pull at my face in the mirror every morning because I didn't recognize who was staring back at me. Have you ever felt that way? Truly unsure who that person was looking back? I didn't like what I saw and couldn't understand what I should be anymore. So I thought about it long and hard and wrestled it for months. I knew without a shadow of a doubt only one person in my life would get it—would be able to understand my atrocious lack of self worth and frustration and loss. I wasn't the confident, jolly, adventurous Alec Stone anymore that everyone else knew. That's why I called you. I knew you would get it. Maybe I was too hard on you with this whole thing. It's a huge burden to bear. But I thought if anyone got why I *really* left Michigan it should be you," he belabored.

"Why me? Why would I get it?" I asked, puzzled.

"Because after Jez broke your heart, I saw the same lifelessness in your eyes that I was seeing every time I looked into the mirror. I heard the same melancholic sighs all too often, for no apparent reason. I could perceive the exhaustion in your words. She blew your candle out and you lost your light for a little bit. And for the past little while, so did I. That's how I knew you would understand more than anyone else I knew," he finished.

"Honestly, and I mean that—no white lies about it, you just described exactly how it felt. Sometimes, how it still feels. I didn't realize in all my despair that you were struggling so badly, too. I'm so sorry I missed it. I really am," I croaked, emotionally.

"Next time, we both need to step up to the plate. But Jacobs, if I have my way, there won't be a next time ever again. After this debacle of a getaway is over, hopefully we'll both find the right girl, the ones we've always dreamt about, the type that is striking, educated, intoxicating, and makes us want to settle down," he said. "I believe here today, even with only a sliver of evidence, that we will find something worth settling down with," he finished. They were powerful words from a powerless man, flapping his gums around ravenously, looking half-crazy. With that, he turned on his heel to the corridor marked east. Not a word was spoken the remainder of the night leaving the words hanging out in outer space to be mixed in with a multitude of emotions. Nothing was clear except that it would be my responsibility to change Alec's mind about going back to Florida to seek unvarnished vindication.

Across Cobbled Alleys

Chapter 14

I pictured her in a yellow dress, her silhouette illuminated under the tented lawn by the dusky orange glow cast from the sunset. She turned her head to the side, gracing all of those around her with a smile, tilting her head down toward her shoulder sweetly, glancing around at her friends and instantly, I was drunk off her poise. It felt as if I had known her a thousand years, touched her a thousand times, but I still couldn't make out her face clearly. I stood 100 yards away, sauntering too slowly like walking through sinking sand, the weight of the air held me down for my own good toward her curves. As I drew near, my eyes glossed over into black and I awoke with a gasp.

"Anna? What are you doing here?" I asked excitedly.

Before I could distinguish if it was Anna, Stone woke me up with a whoosh!

"Wake up man. We need to talk. Look, I'm sorry about last night, I might've said some stuff I didn't need to say. I figured out what we need to do. You might not like the answer but hear me out first," Alec was wide-awake.

"It's all good man. In the heat of the moment, sometimes we all lose our cool. But seriously, what time is it? I was having a hell of a good dream."

"The time is not important, my friend. What is important is the fact that I have marinated on our conversation from last night. Let's go to Callie's wedding," he beamed enthusiastically.

"You mean it? How are you so sure? Last night you were unsure at even the proposition," I replied.

"I knew you were right. There are many reasons to go, I stand by what I said last night, but her wedding, that ephemeral experience is the root of all of this madness inside of me," Stone said.

"Hell yes! It is a once in a lifetime. Let's make ourselves present in this paramount moment. Maybe it'll bring the closure necessary for you to really move on, Stone" I began to wake up from pure, unfiltered excitement.

"I can hope so. I really do hope so. When do you want to head back to Florida, Turner?" He asked.

"You say when. I'm ready whenever. But I have to ask, what about Chelsea? Where does she fit into this mess?

"I see myself with two or three legitimate options. One, I take her with me. She's a good-looking girl. Rich. Well put together. That would definitely sting Callie a little bit. Two, I leave right now as not to hurt her even more than I would if she came with me, and reconvene with that girl Ellie. She's right on the way, in Mississippi now matter of fact. She goes to college over there. So I see that as an opportunistic option. And lastly, option three, maybe the best option, drop everything and find someone at the wedding to make my own for the night," he stared ahead smugly as if he presented the best argument one had ever heard.

"I can tell you've really thought this through man," I laughed. Have you even made mention to Chelsea about Callie's wedding?"

"Not really. She doesn't need to know about my messy past. It's called the past for a reason, Jacobs," Alec said.

"Can we really consider it past when it still lingers on in the present?" I jabbed playfully. "I don't want to decide for you. What does your gut say?" I questioned, passively.

"You're a comedian now, are you? You might want to stick to your day job, Jacobs. My gut says Ellie. Fresh blood could be good. Even though she's not exactly fresh blood because I've had her before, as I mentioned earlier," he said cockily.

"She moved to Mississippi with her family for college last year if I recall. You know she knows Callie, right? And Anna? She's *probably* be going to the wedding already, any way," I replied, reflecting on text messages she and I had already exchanged a several weeks back.

"I know she's going to wedding. I talked to her about it a little while back. I haven't caught up with her lately, so I can't say for a fact she's still going, though," he replied, as if I should have already known this information.

"She's basically best friends with Callie's younger sister. I'm pretty sure she'll go," I stated.

164

"She always had it bad for me," he reflected.

"Then what happened between the two of you if she had it so *hot* for you?" I pushed.

"Callie, man. Callie is what happened. When you meet the girl of your fucking dreams, even the best looking girl you've ever dated cannot hold a candle to her and the feeling she gives you down deep in your lovely bones. Nothing can beat that feeling," Stone said.

"The sweet taste of love, or what we determine to be love, is unparalleled man. So what are you going to do about Chelsea? Are you sure your mind is up made up about picking up Ellie? The wedding is in three days. You need to call her. This is a now or never situation," I stated.

"You leave that to me. Just give me the day," he declared confidently.

"You got it. Do you need my help? I don't want this to be a disaster," I uttered, thinking out loud.

"Nah. I think I know more about breaking hearts than you do, Turner Jacobs."

And with that, he whisked away into the early morning light and I grabbed my phone and dialed in her number, regardless of what Alec said. Sometimes I knew better than him. This was one of those occasions.

"Ellie?"

"Hey Turner! What's up? She giggled.

"Kind of what we expected. It looks like we're going to Callie's wedding after all. Are you still going to go? Would you want to join us?" I asked

"Yay! Of course I'm going. I thought you would never call, I didn't think Alec would end up going. I asked him about going as my date a few months ago, and he never got back with me," she exclaimed.

"He went back and forth about it for some time, but now he really wants to go. It's taken some time, but I'm pretty sure he's over Callie. Your name keeps coming up in our conversations," I replied.

"I hope he's over her! He is going to love the dress I bought. It's silver and sheen and really kind of sexy if I say so myself," she charmed.

"I bet you'll look amazing. Sorry, I have to go but I'll let you know when we're on our way tomorrow. We'll probably arrive early evening," I mentioned.

"I'm so excited! See y'all tomorrow!" she closed.

"Me too, Ell. See you later."

***

The constellations were so bright they nearly moaned in the night sky as Desi and I walked around Highland Park. We always enjoyed walking together, finding it to be a time where we could air our feelings sans judgment. For some reason, the peace of the outdoors gave the illusion of acceptance, as if all the green grass and bushy trees bowed at their knees and welcomed our conversations.

"I still miss James Ryan," she said softly as we rounded the corner of the block.

"I know you do. Have you heard from him at all? Have you tried to contact him?" I mused.

"No, not really. He'll text me stuff now and again, but nothing important. I don't know why I thought he was different. He seemed so different than the others," she said.

"They all seem different at first, Des. After a considerable amount of time, if they keep coming back to you and you want to stay glued to their side, that's how you know they are actually different," I replied.

"I am sick of the bullshit and of being fooled into believing in people who aren't worth believing in," she sighed under the glow of dusky orange streetlights.

"Me too, Des. I know someone is coming for you. You're far too wonderful a catch for no one equally magnetic to catch you," I smiled.

"I love you, brother. I can't wait to see where we will end up," she stopped, grabbing me and lunged in for a hug.

"I love you too. I always will," I hugged her tiny body. No matter her physical size, she was always my little sister who I still pictured as a toddler at times.

"Are you ready to head back to Florida to wrap this adventure up, Turner? It sure has been longer and more widespread than I ever could have imagined when I agreed to join you," she added.

"More than I ever thought I would be. I'm starting to miss home. It's not a perfect place, but we keep seeing more places and it seems that they all have quirks. They all have things I love and thing I despise. In each place we have gone, I've experienced miracles and struggles. I realized we might as well be where we have family and friends to endure those struggles and strife with, communally."

She thought about my words slowly, staring off toward a large red brick home that sat on the corner of Chelsea's street.

"It's that simple? It all breaks down to that?" She asked.

"Maybe it does. Maybe it doesn't. I hope that's what it is. There's no wrong answer but to give up. The key is to keep pushing yourself so that you keep making progress. Complacency is the greatest of evils," I assured her.

"Won't you get complacent back home? You seemed to be rather bored before. Sometimes I feel terribly listless there, too," she reflected.

"It could happen again. But this time, I swear it is my greatest goal to put effort into not being complacent. It's partly a choice and I'm choosing to live limitlessly. God knows our plans and He made all of our lives from day one to day end, after all. So after

168

the wedding, I'll head home to see what the great sea of life has to offer me," I said as we returned to Chelsea's driveway. "Don't ever change. I love how deeply you think about things. I usually don't think about what is going to happen tomorrow. But lately, being with you and Alec and everyone, I feel that changing within me. Let's pack up. We have another mountain to conquer this week and we better get to it," she said as we entered the house and parted ways for the night.

In a short walk around an unknown, upscale Texas neighborhood, I witnessed the first step of the transformation of Desi from child to adult. As much as I tried to push the emotions away, I felt proud from head to toe and tears welled in my eyes. She was always a breathe of fresh air compared to the messy, smoggy existence of others, and I was starting to notice she was beginning to see her new budding potential even in moments of defeat.

Across Cobbled Alleys

Chapter 15

Just as soon as Texas began, it ended. Alec's masterful plan wasn't much of a plan at all. We snuck out and packed all of our things in the middle of the night and left. He had the conscience of a squirrel. My conscience, on the other hand, was overwhelmed for leaving Chelsea's home unannounced to a single soul. I felt a sense of obligation to her for some reason. My soul owed her great gratitude for her hopeful, ambitious nature that was striving only towards finding love.

Once again, my tires felt the burden of travel and Stone slept in the seat next to me. I thought on how I loved everyone I could not, and that was just the way it seemed to work. Maybe it'll be different, maybe I've changed—or the female species has changed or we've both changed and we'll meet for some paradise tipped adventure together in authentic purgatory; Earth.

Stone shook his head in his sleep and rocked himself right awake. He looked over puzzled, confused, and raised his mouth slightly into a forced smile. Five minutes later, he broke the verbal silence.

"What on earth is to come of us man?" Alec moaned.

"What do you mean, buddy?"

170

"Well, all this traveling—the miles—the days—the cities—they all bleed together into one huge blob on the floor. It's all a different version of the same. The South, the North—their divide is as much rooted in the weeping willows of Savannah's past—not present in the present, but existing only in memory. It only breathes new life through people recalling things they weren't even alive to see, or to know about," he sighed heavily, tracing the car windowsill. He broke a mad sweat of poetic rhythm when he rambled.

"Would you rather not see it all? Sure, it's shades of the same gray, but remiss we would be if we didn't taste each place's own taste on our own. Don't know about you, Alec, but I need to taste it all. Here, there—Mississippi and California and Montana and all of the places in between. I need to taste them for my own senses sake."

"Right, you're right. I know that's all true. I'm just starting to see how small this far-too large world really can be. Still, I am not sure where I'll end up...or with whom. And what in the hell I'll be doing there? That's just another fragment of the unknown," he said quizzically.

"The unknowing can make it all the more beautiful," I replied.

A phone rang out blaringly breaking the silence, cutting the conversation short. Sometimes in all his infinite talky-talk, Alec could fall into a wallow laden depressive ramble. And regardless of who you were, you would be bulled over by the anvil of his sadness. The shrill, high-pitched voice on the other line was none other than Ellie. She talked hopeful and immature, like a child, because frankly, at age 19, that's what she was. But she would never succumb to that realization. She was a contributing member of this society in her own brain space. Not more than a handful of days past her 19th birthday, she had kept periodic correspondence with Stone after our fateful, drunken beach encounter a year prior.

"When'll y'all arrive?" She squawked. Alec enjoyed Ellie as a human being, but he loathed her voice. Her voice didn't mirror her beautiful exterior. I agreed, and would've have put a pacifier in her mouth if I had the option.

"Sorry we're running a little later than we thought. You still going to fix us a meal?" Stone laughed, rolling his eyes and smacking my forearm. He loved to be an enhanced, spectacularly peculiar version of himself when it came to Ellie. Maybe it was the age discrepancy, maybe it was the cultural variations between the two, but either way, Stone channeled something uniquely invigorating in his relationship with Ellie. They drove each other up the walls wild. It had cataclysmic written all over it.

"That'd be your dream come true, wouldn't it, Alec? Anna, my other friend y'all met at the beach is here and we are busy getting ready."

"It'd be the dream for sure," he murmured.

172

"Yea, we'll see you soon. I should go shower," she replied.

"Or you could just wait and do it with me?" Stone joked, but laced with utter seriousness.

"Slow your roll there, Alec," she sternly spoke back.

"What? C'mon, I was only kidding."

"Uh-huh, you were kidding. Sure, I believe *that*," she emphasized the last word with glee.

"Okay, so maybe I wasn't...."

"Ha! I knew it, you perv. But I'm really going to go shower now. We'll see y'all soon," and she hung up before he could get another retort into the conversation.

"Anna is there, Jacobs! How about that for irony? Of all people in the whole damn world, Anna is there with Ellie," Alec chuckled with tears flowing from his eyes.

"What are you talking about? Anna from the beach?" I asked, shocked.

"According to Ellie, they are getting ready for us to pick them up and roll to the wedding after all. Amazing are God's plans," he said shaking his head optimistically.

I wondered if God had *anything* to do with this plan. Was this a disaster waiting to happen? Time would reveal that answer all too soon.

Before either of us knew it, we were entering the one-stop light town of Meridian, Mississippi. Covered with brick buildings on Main Street, which was indeed the town's "main" street, Meridian had avoided most of the corporatization that America had been overwhelmed with the past few decades. It was entirely draped in Southern charm and hospitality. The town itself, reminiscent of the 1950's, couldn't help but welcome you into its wide-open arms.

"What in the world have we gotten ourselves into?" Alec mused as his eyes wandered the streets that would've been filled with churchgoers and other citizens rambling and fanning their faces from the incredibly penetrating sunshine any given Sunday. His pupils grew and his eyes paced anxiously around the towns four corners.

"Thank God for AC," I moaned.

Stone's phone rang and rang again. Every person in the car knew it was Chelsea that was calling, and Alec couldn't bring himself to grow up and answer the phone call.

"Stone, you really should just answer it and tell her what's up. Just tell her you're sorry," Desi nudged.

"Hell no! There's literally nothing I can say that is a valid excuse for leaving in the middle of the night with no explanation, no goodbye, no note," he scoffed.

I wish he had thought of that previously.

"You owe her at least an apology. She was really good to all of us, especially you," Desi pushed.

Still, Stone let the phone ring and ring until finally I summoned the courage to answer it for him.

"Hey Chelsea, what's up?" I said as Alec's face drained to a shade of cloud white. I could hear her whimpering on the other end of the line.

"What the heck is going on? Why did y'all just up and go? Who the heck does that?" She wailed.

"I wish I had told you sooner, but I have a wedding to attend in Florida. I wasn't leaving because of you. I'm sorry I didn't give you any kind of proper notice," I said, pretending to be Alec Stone. Strangely enough, perhaps because she didn't discern it to be my voice over her yelps and wails, she continued as if she was talking to Alec.

"A wedding? A freaking wedding? Why wouldn't you ask me to come? I can't begin to understand you, Alec Stone. I knew you were too good to be true. I can't believe I almost gave up my virginity to you. I should've known better after that situation at the beach with that Blythe girl," she roared.

"I know, I know. I'm a son of a bitch. I'm really sorry. How close did we get again? Really close, right?" I chided as Alec's face contorted to display his agitation.

"You pig! I hate you! I *seriously* hate you! And I wasn't raised to talk like that, but you Alec Stone, are one of those horrible bastards Daddy always warned me about. I hope you have fun at your stupid wedding. And never, ever, for any reason, contact me again," she screamed.

"I can explain, really, please me a chance..."

"You lost your chance. I'm sorry I ever believed you when you said you wanted to be with me. I'm sorry I'm that stupid. Talk to you never, Alec," she slammed the phone down and the line went blank.

"Wow, there's a new number one on the Alec Stone list of enemies," I roared.

"Ha, laugh it up guys! I feel terrible about the whole thing. That Chelsea, despite what she just said, is a very nice girl. I wish it could've worked," he said it so caustically. Almost no fear on his face since the conversation abruptly ended.

"Do you think you'll ever hear from her again?" Desi asked.

"I know I will. They always come back around. Sometimes it's for one more shot, or to take one more shot at you, but either way, she'll contact me again," he stated like a man seasoned with similar experiences.

The heat was a buzz kill for my adventurous side, leaving me ready to cool off in a country basement infused with snow cold air—all lied up with a pretty girl—no mind if it meant anything to either of us. And as the southern evening air stuck heavy as smog on our skin, we exited the township to the North, to the country, and two girls desirous of our company (or at least we tried to believe that) awaited our nearing arrival. Knots grew in my stomach and I had that feeling where you want to disappear, poof into thin air—but there was no going back.

We pulled up to the small, gray house fitted with the essential wrap around porch, and an enormous barn converted into a garage on the western portion of the property. As it played out many times before, we were met with jovial faces and jubilance. Even if it was becoming expected, it was absolutely refreshing each and every time, in each and all of the places. Because no one wants to be a complete stranger, seemingly lost and looking for another destination all the time. We all expect the acceptance of a familiar face. And in this instance, there were two staring right back at us. The knots in my stomach grew at the sight of her...yellow dress, beaming smile and all, just the way I pictured her in my sweet dream! The riot on my insides pinged from vein to vein and the wayward journey, at long last, made sense.

***

Stale pretzels were my breakfast as blue birds woke me from lightest slumber. It felt like I'd slept an hour or two, despite the reality I'd slept nearly ten. Stone was still asleep, rolled into a fetal position ball, next to me in the small queen bed in Ellie's basement. Quite a change from our previous digs at Chelsea's Texas McMansion. Ellie's home was welcoming, yet dingy, in coexistence. The basement consisted of an entertainment room marked by cement walls and a large worn plaid covered couch, looking well utilized by the impressions left happily in the cushions.

The entertainment room led to the laundry room, then a bathroom. The bathroom was white tiled room with no color to it at all, with a smell of summer cotton and fresh cut lemon. Finally, at the east end of the basement was the guest room. The guest room featured a dated, antique dresser made of early 1900's oak. A matching queen headboard accompanied a worn mattress, the one her parents had when they were first married, which marred the comfort we felt sleeping on it, and a worn white side table sat next to the bed. It had an over sized Ikea analog alarm clock on it. The kind with numbers that are so brazenly red, and so large, they're engrained in your mind when you think of the time of day it was, no matter where you were.

What is it about the eyes first examination of morning that seems so foreign? The wandering pupils dash and dart across the light that illuminates what was and should be a dark room. Life, morning, and its innocent light are like finding love; we always wonder in the darkness if the effulgent glow of light will come once again. And we hope with whatever lies beneath our skin that it does exist and that no matter where we are— they will all commence and it'll all be alright and our day will be blessed with something or someone meaningful.

Stone finally emerged from the room to find the girls both entirely asleep, and wandered uncomfortably toward the kitchen of Ellie's house, which we had never seen before. Still buzzing from the night before, Stone stepped out the slider door to smoke a cigar. I stretched my arms like a jet, merely stretching, but looking ready to take flight. Clouds were rolling quickly due east, but the sun's rays snuck through. Cross-eyed, my pupils sought the skyline. Stone was giddy and I could tell just from the creases in his cheeks and his puffed out chest that he had a fulfilling night.

He kept clamoring on about how this was going to be one hell of a week and how Ellie was the one he had been looking for. How could he not see it before? Did he use the other girls as decoys? I thought to myself while Stone murmured on. I reiterated how great Ellie was, saying what my best friend wanted to hear, only thinking about everything else under the sun. Especially Anna Bishop. Alec was in and out, hot and cold. We both laughed weakly, swept with morning faces and glow of sleep.

"How was last night?" He asked.

"Not bad, still trying to figure her out."

"She's a tricky one that's for sure. But if anyone can solve that mystery, it's Turner Jacobs, legendary female connoisseur that came to life during our college days," he bellowed.

"Who's that? I can hardly remember that son of a bitch. Almost a former life kind of thing," I sighed.

"Come on. That's ridiculous, just bloody absurd. Maybe you've hit a speed bump since Jez, but it's just that—a mere speed bump. Once the wheels get rolling and you allow yourself to ease off your self imposed brakes—then you'll know you still have it. They better watch out, I swear." He offered me exactly what I had needed to hear spoken. The power of hearing something meaningful, and the presence of human flesh-ness providing those sentences—there is a grand form of beauty within that which quells fear.

"Thanks man. Time will tell. This Anna excites me," I stated.

"As she should, my friend," he remarked. "Shall we find breakfast?" He smiled and I nodded in full agreement as we approached Ellie's square box room with a sense of secretive urgency, looking not to be discovered by the rest of the people in the house just yet.

The girls, down-home and Southern, prepared a feast of scrambled eggs, grits, bacon and orange juice. No mind that neither of us liked grits, we gobbled up each bite like it was the last piece of food available on Earth. While we ate the delicious meal, the kitchen fell silent and eight eyes wandered the tiny kitchens confines. Fifteen minutes later, Anna began rambling on about something, which I couldn't understand, showcasing her naivety and the discrepancy between our ages, as Ellie snuck

Alec back to her bedroom. I listened to each word she said and attempted to seek purpose in her ramblings about dramatic things I wouldn't have understood even if we had been the same age. We came from two distinctly different worlds. She complained and awkwardly hopped from one subject to another and all I really wanted to do was hold her body closer. That's the strange thing about being a nice guy. The nice guy—both dynamic and nurturing, is void of being seen as sexual by most of the females they spend time with. The nicer a guy is to a girl, his chances of sleeping with her drop dramatically. Hell, the chances of him being involved with her romantically are diminished just as significantly. I hated that facet of being who I was—it made no sense to me. We so called nice guys are busy loving the loveless and so the loveless we remain. And from the first time those words reached my ears, I knew it was impossible to forget.

As I continued to love the loveless, Stone was *making* it, as the entire house could hear the oft kilter moans and groans. "Thank God her father isn't here to hear that," I rolled my eyes toward Anna.

"Alec won't have to worry about that. He's gone," she said whispering.

"What do you mean, gone?"

"He left her mama about a month ago. Said this life just wasn't working for him anymore. So he moved out west, I think, to someplace like Colorado."

"Wow," I said in disbelief. "That's really rough. She must be going through some serious stuff right now."

"Not really. She's fine. Just listen to her right now," innocence dribbled away bit by bit from Anna's lips since our initial encounter. And I liked her less because of it. So, naturally, she liked me more. It had been this way since I was a bright-eyed boy of fifteen and it remained this way until forever met the sunset. Unabashedly, Anna placed her hand above my knee on my overpriced, broken-in AG jeans.

"Do you wanna, you know?" She bit her lips slow, watching each tooth press into her bottom lip, anticipation building as I grasped her soft soaked flesh, "Want to go downstairs?"

"Don't ask twice," I rushed out. The angel and devil on my shoulder grabbed their violins and played me two songs, distinct in nature, but I chose to hear neither and grabbed her elegant slender fingers and led her down the stairway. And just as Stone above me, a euphoric, intimate, and sacred excursion began. And to this day, a man of many second-guessing's, but few regrets, I stand entirely filled with happiness—soft and gentle as first snow—when that night wanders back to my ever-dream drowned brain. Because that day, from sun-up until sundown changed the course of all the days that would follow. Isn't that some kind of bizarre? One simple 24 hour blip, a dot on a screen, a speck of sand at the lakeside, what if these micro moments could impact every other portion of days and segments around them? Believe me, they can. And they will.

As the sun slowly sunk, all I wanted to do was lie in the metaphorical meadow, knee deep in some kind of celestial love as the crickets sang merrily on and I'm not constrained for time or space at all. Bliss can only be found when our concept of time is completely destroyed. It took time, no pun intended, but I was coming to realize it surely. And as we waded together knee deep in the meadow, jeans and bare feet happy as an oyster—I decided to deconstruct the almighty watch that all humans allow to hang above their forehead, ticking beat by beat obnoxiously. There was a change in the winds stirring me toward her—and the realization that action and inaction are both *actually* actions. There's great, sincere, enormous knowledge in inaction. At times it is equally as important as taking action. And if my steps are planned for me anyway, my inaction was perfect. And necessary. Just like every other thing I've ever done and ever will do. All quilt pieces woven in God's great tapestry of life. And all strung up were my memories, like telephone wires, standing along the highways and back roads of my heart. This night would be the pulse, the frequency that kept me buzzing. I was enamored with her, struck by her unmatched beauty.

"Anna, do you believe each person has a soul mate?" I asked her while staring at the popcorn ceiling.

"I don't know, but I hope so. I know it sounds dorky or whatever, but I've always hoped that each person has a perfect match," she replied back honestly.

"I hope so too," I replied, content with not being asked a question in return.

She rolled on her pretty side and I watched as the moon glittered her face and her eyes danced step for step with mine.

"If it's out there, true love and all of that, I hope that you are able to find it, Anna. Don't sell yourself short for anyone. Somebody's going to be luckier than life," I stated, trying to deflect interest in her because I was so unsure of myself at the time.

"He's out there, Turner. And I have not a single doubt that when the time is right, he'll find me," she replied confidently.

"I couldn't agree more pretty girl. When the time is right, the right guy will arrive. I bet when you least expect it."

Across Cobbled Alleys

Chapter 16

Assisting Alec Stone with his tie, I put on a seersucker sport coat and dress slacks, though it was quite warm for this type of attire, as we prepared to attend the girls' local cotillion event. It was an old Southern tradition, with whiskey, malt liqueur and the best wines known to mankind, flowing voraciously. Not that I enjoyed much of the above, but I liked seeing other people enjoy them. Some a bit too much, but my enjoyment dissipated scarcely.

"Alec, we can only stay tonight. We have to leave tomorrow. Do you hear me?" I shouted from the dance floor.

"Yeah, sure I got you, Jacobs," he said coyly as he danced by with Ellie on his arm.

"I know how you get wrapped up in this stuff. We can't lose track of time. Tomorrow morning we have to be on our way," I yelled joyously.

"You got it, big guy. On our way to the sunshine state in the morning..." Stone replied, drink in his left hand while his right hand rested on Ellie's curvaceous butt.

Stone and Ellie were intoxicatingly engrossed with one another; dancing, twirling, and spinning around like a carousel on the white-tented floor. They looked more in love than I knew was possible this soon. Her sky blue gown dazzled in the dim light and her skin was ripe-orange tan, life filled and lovable was she. It was no wonder Alec was flipping his bananas at the idea of having little miss thing to call his own. Making my night all the more complex was Anna's ex-boyfriend, whose name I can't recall—lurking around the party, eyeing Anna and I with snake eyes. She still loved him—in that pathetic, sad puppy dog way that we all long for our first love after it's clearly over—and he had used her puppy dog sadness to keep her around. It's bizarre, but after seeing him gawk at her all night, awe struck by her body, desirous of her very flesh, made a fire burn in my stomach. With each of his glances, growing longer each time, my desire for her fervently grew within my chest. I couldn't stop myself—so I approached her with a swagger more cognizant of confidence than arrogance.

"Anna?" sweetly I spoke to her.

"Yes, Turner?"

"Would you do me the honor of another dance?"

She smiled, blushed hot tamale red and grabbed my outstretched hand and we approached the floor quickly. Life is so much about the dance and what a strange, beautiful dance it can be. When we're willing to give in and let our bodies drop into gravity as if we can float, our flowing, frolicking, and for me, flailing bodies all around the sweltering summer night. At once, every worry I had was dismissed. My brain could go from over drive to neutral and remain there for a while. It reminded me of the "mental health" days my mother gave us as children to skip school once a year. How I longed for those days with the birds chirping, lemonade sipping, and sweet and slow afternoons playing cards with my mother. Those days were free, like dancing. And on that cotillion evening, so was I.

Storms rolled in over the Mississippi Delta and the lightning fluidly washed yellow across the previously quiet night sky. Blobs of rain, more drops than drips, kissed our skin as we ran amongst the shallow field to our parked car. And at that moment, I saw how much fun we were having on this expedition. I finally saw what Stone had so desperately wanted to see this whole time; we were all genuinely living! We were living in the here, in the now, in the moment completely. No longer living in confliction with our happiness, we embraced our happiness in every aspect of our lives from sun up to sun down. When such a splendorous and magnificent feeling finds you, there's little left to search for. Goose bumps and yelps of wild and weird jubilation, your youth is what you make it in your mind and happiness is the same. Stone was showing me this, chasing and clawing towards it with each slither and step. Now that he almost had it, he was sharing this piece of influential wisdom with us all just by the carefree way he was trying to live.

To top off an already perfect evening, Anna grabbed my hand as we entered Ellie's house. She smiled, giddy, and whispered the four words any and all red-blooded men love to hear: "I want you now." And touched by her, I touched her, and the night played on beautifully. Untying her dress, it fell in a heap on the floor around her taut ankles. I was already down to the boxer briefs and my undershirt anyway. Her hands, with spaghetti slender fingers, clasped my hips and I began to kiss her neck softly, sweetly. Slipping under satin summertime sheets were our natural canvases, plain and unfinished. We spent the entire A.M. hours painting, creating, and making our own work of art. Our hidden affairs echoed the four walls loudly, but only the moon caught a glimpse of our encounter. It was definitively magical, and equally serene, the bodies becoming one in a spectacular unison that one cannot buy with all of the cursed money ever invented.

After our sweetest and longest dance of the night, I contemplated if it had to be our last. We had Callie's wedding to attend tomorrow. I was bone chillingly hopeful as her supple butterfly lips kissed my sinful face and I knew I wouldn't let any piece of this memory get deleted from my archive. No, this was a forever memory loved away in my treasure chest if I had anything to say about it.

***

The sex was encompassing and magnificent to the point that I dreamt about it further that night. In my dreams, I asked God above if my intentions were worth even a copper penny in this wishing well life? He shook his head at me. Crickets surrounded us in the field surrounding the house and I lead her to the path near the barn. And beginning to make my exit, lickity split trying to run away from love, her aqua green eyes took me over, possessed my fragile heart in them, and we were hand in hand. But the ethereal glow in her, beaming like the Fourth of July fireworks across the sky in my mind, was too undeniable to just ignore. Strawberry wine on our lips, clothes worse for the wear, we looked around at all the glory in the evening hours and prayed no one would stumble upon our half-naked scene. She played country music from her phone that I didn't care for much, but it wasn't going to kill the mood on a night too effulgent to contain our emotions in its grips. Consequently, we let our bodies talk for hours. In the end of the dream, all went to black except for a gold glittering light glitzing on and off in the corner of my view. Are you still there, God? He flashed three times as if to tell me He was, is and always will be. I had to trust that He wouldn't mislead me. I couldn't escape the feeling as I exited her room that I left her inside her own nightmare howl hell darkness where all muddy and unclear things exist in a rumination of black by loving her and fleeing the scene.

With a jolt, I awoke and looked over at the analog Ikea alarm clock that read 6:57 A.M. I hadn't talked to Christ in my waking moments in awhile and decided it was more than time to do so, as Anna lied next to me smiling in her sleep. "Jesus, protect me from myself. Please don't allow me to fail again. For you are God, so who am I to get lost in the age of my worry? I get scared by the unknown, but the future being unknown is a part of the whole deal. Let me be the believer I know I am. Let me be cleansed by your love that is more than capable of washing away the stupid sins of my flesh. Do not let me reflect poorly on your name. Amen!"

Two hours later, everyone was awake, even Desi, who had been relegated to sidebar conversation with people that she didn't know for two straight days. I felt bad for her because Stone and I were all tied up with the girls and she sat idly by. She was so kind for waiting, even dog sitting during cotillion the night prior, but her patience was beginning to wear thin. None of us knew quite what to expect when we actually arrived in Florida.

I carried Anna's things, Alec carried Ellie's and all three girls prepared a cooler of snacks, water and beer for the road. Alec had a twinkle in his eye I hadn't seen since things were truly good with Callie. As we packed the car, again, which was beginning to feel like a recurring dream, he chuckled to himself. "What?" I asked.

190

"I don't know Turner. What am I doing? There's not a thing I can say that would make Callie want me back," he laughed out loud.

"But do you even want her? Isn't this more finding a crystal clear sense of closure? You seem pretty damn thrilled about Ellie right now, any way it seems," I said.

"I don't know what it's about any more. When we left I thought I needed to get her back. But now, on this wild ass journey, I've learned innumerable things about myself, especially these past few weeks. I don't need her back, Turner. Whether it's with Ellie or on my own, I'm going to be okay. It's all going to be okay," relief could be seen in his smile lines.

"I know you are. I knew it all along," I chided.

Moments later, the girls came out and piled into the car for the final seven-hour drive to Florida for Callie and Kip's wedding. The tension in the car was thick as smog and we tuned it out by turning the music up.

"Does Callie know who you are bringing to the wedding?" I asked Ellie.

"She doesn't know, but her sister Jane is one of my best friends from back home. They're such a chill family that they wont care who I bring," she relayed.

"You didn't happen to mark plus 1 on your RSVP, did you?" Desi joked.

"Actually I did. I was still with my ex when I replied, so I think I marked two people on the card," she said as we all laughed.

"What about you, Anna?" Stone asked.

"Same here. I RSVP'd that two guests would be coming because I was still with that fat son of a bitch of a boyfriend of mine when I got the invitation," she said, blowing air out of her nostrils.

"So in theory, Desi is the only truly uninvited guest. I guess I could split my meal with you," I joked, jabbing playfully at my sister.

"Hey now! Callie always loved me. Well, that is, the five times I actually saw her she loved me at least," she added.

"Yeah, she was a big fan of yours actually," Stone piped up.

"Really? I always knew she had awesome taste," she laughed, darting her eyes at Stone.

"I think you are forgetting a few things... like when she cheated on me with Kip for the last three months we were dating. That wasn't exactly something I would describe as awesome," he said acting upset.

"I know I know. I'm only playing of course," Desi replied.

"Desi, what made you want to come down here to bum fuck Mississippi or Texas or wherever y'all have been?" Anna posed.

"It would take me days to tell you the whole ordeal, seriously, but mostly because I wanted to see something new. I wanted to go somewhere I hadn't seen before. It was probably partly to see if love was really out there, or to support Turner and Alec. I don't really know, but I don't even care. Meeting all of these new people, everything has been a blast," Desi replied.

192

"That's cool. I love meeting new people. Once I went to summer camp, and I developed like *way* before all the other girls and all of the boys at the camp were trying to mess around and do things with me! It was exciting at first but got seriously annoying after awhile," Anna giggled, speaking like a girl turned woman at too young an age.

"Well you're hot, girl! Obviously guys were trying to get with you," Desi chirped up.

"Please don't add to her self esteem," Ellie added.

"Bitch, what ever. My self esteem isn't even high in the first place," Anna smiled sheepishly.

"Well you wanna know what I think?" Desi asked.

"We're all hot as heck and any guy out there in the universe would be lucky to spend time with us. So take note boys, you are in some elite company," Desi poked, staring toward Alec and I.

"We are as lucky as the day is long," Stone spoke up.

"Couldn't have said it better myself, Alec," I added for good measure with a childlike smile at Anna.

We arrived into the sunshine state in the dusky cotton candy layered haze of evening and grabbed two hotel rooms two miles from the reception hall. The girls had a room and the guys had a room, which I found interesting, because Alec was chomping at behind close doors with Ellie. I wished to spend some more time with Anna, also, but my best friend needed me far more than she did that night. Poor Desi got lost in translation again, forced to stay with Ellie and Anna. After Desi and Anna bonded during their several hours scrunched together in the car, they were both excited to share a hotel room. Stone brushed his teeth aggressively, as if to scrub every last stain and scrap of food that ever entered his mouth, used the bathroom, and took the bed nearest the window. I followed with a similar ritual, but scrubbed much less aggressively.

"What you going to say to Callie?"

"All along in my head I have had this elaborate plan to spill my feelings and expound on our past and all of this, but I've been thinking a lot about it like I said. What kind of asshole would I be if I did that? She would never forget it. I don't want to mar her wedding day. I do want to go, I want to see her there and have her see me. Maybe she will see it as some kind of peace offering even. I don't really know," Alec stated maturely.

"After all of this time, it finally has become clear to you hasn't it?" I replied, genuinely proud.

"I think so. It's like God is willing my heart to find peace in my hurt. I really believe He wouldn't let me down. I know my actions have probably let Him down lately. In fact, I know they have. I'll change one day. I just don't know if I am entirely ready to change yet. But I feel it in my veins Turner—one day I am going to change my not so intentional wicked ways," he murmured.

"He is peace and He brings peace. Just not always in the timetable that we ask for it. I try to remember that all the time,

194

but it is a lot easier to say it to you than to follow it myself," I said earnestly.

"Isn't that the truth? We really ought to get some sleep," Alec said, turning out his bedpost light.

"Goodnight man."

"Night, Stone," I replied.

And while the suggestion to arrive at the actual wedding had been mine in the first place, in hindsight it was clear that Alec needed to see her again. To see her happy as she ever was, even if it wasn't with him, so that he could finally let go of her forever. Maybe this most enormous of occasions would finally ease the pain and anger he had been he had carried on his back for a year and a half. I hoped it for my friend with all my being. He wasn't a way ward cowboy, even if he appeared that way over and over again since losing her. It was losing her that brought out this presumptuous and absurd behavior in the first place. Adventurer? Sure. Ruthless heartbreaker? No. I felt it in my bones that we were only a handful of hours away from realizing Alec Stone was going to be fine after all. The room fell silent before one last effort to put the past precisely where it belonged... undoubtedly behind him.

Across Cobbled Alleys

Chapter 17

Stone had paced the hotel for over an hour, eating a blueberry muffin and sipping coffee passively out of a paper cup. The girls occupied the bathroom with curling iron and hair straighter wires crisscrossed all over the small space. Towels, make up bags and dresses were messily spread all over the floor. I decided to lie in bed just a little while longer. Spiders climbed my soul while anxiety set deeply into me for my best friend. I imagined myself in a similar position. Even after all of those years, and many people who had come and gone from the mystery of my movie life, it would still have caused me to breakdown. I couldn't handle seeing my ex in the flesh ever again. Stone appeared bipolar, as he stood scared and stiff, yet equally free-floating around the room. He kept smiling, but not in a nervous fashion. It was an impressive performance to say the least.

I finally got up and quickly readied myself in khakis, a checkered Lacoste shirt and navy blue blazer. Stone put on linen looking white pants and a purple and yellow short sleeve shirt. I waited outside with Stone, as he puffed away on his cigar. The smoke tracing his lips slowly, he sighed heavily.

196

"Here it goes. If I have to do this, and I know I do, I'm thankful you're here too," he said.

"I wouldn't make you do something like this alone. I have to tell you man, one of the coolest things about you is that you could do it either way. You can handle this whole thing in perfect stride without missing a single beat," I said, trying to infuse his veins with lifeblood and confidence.

"I don't know about that man, but ever since I decided it's not my place to interrupt her most distinct memory, it got a lot easier. I know I have to go and see her in the flesh. Beyond that, truly, I don't see another way to find such definitive open and shut closure, do you?" He asked rhetorically.

"There's no closure like listening to her saying forever to some other guy," I said trying to make light of his rhetorical question.

"I sincerely hope you're able to get closure. It's about time to go, though. Want to holler in to the girls?"

He hollered in and Desi exited first. Anna followed her and lastly, Ellie came out.

The way Alec looked at Ellie was the way every woman longed to be looked at. She was statuesque, her face covered in a powerful purple and her form outlined in the molecules of the sky. She looked like an angel and he was entranced with her every step.

"Let's do this," Anna yelled passionately.

"Wooooo," Desi let out after.

The strawberry sweet air blossomed around the church grounds as the wedding preparations began. The live oaks fell playfully around the windows and canvased the wedding goers from the humidity and brazen sunshine. Cars lined the roads leading up to Holy Waters Pentecostal Church along the coastline of the Gulf of Mexico. We were surprised by the outpouring of people taking part in the destination style wedding initially, only to find out from a cousin at the pre-wedding gathering that Kip's parents were divorced and many of his Mom's side of the family resided nearby. We tried to blend in, but the eyes of others sizzled on our skins as we walked. If I felt so inexplicably noticed, bearing a much more distant connection the wedding, I wondered what Alec Stone was feeling. He did not act agitated for the most part. He strutted with Ellie on his arm and a grin on his face, likely due in part to the four shots of Jose Cuerva tequila he took in our hotel room before our departure.

We joked amongst each other, standing out very little but thinking we stood out like satellites in a dark sky. The bells rang to highlight the four o' clock hour and the people filed into the church one after the other. On a bench across a pathway of cobbled alley sat Alec Stone. His head held in his cupped hands, he moved them to reveal condensation dripping down his face. His hands were windshield wipers for his face, whisking away the tears. I approached him and patted his shoulder.

"You alright man?"

"I can't do this. Why in the hell am I doing this?"

"You're just nervous, and rightfully so. Just relax. This isn't the beginning of another terrible day. This is the brilliantly constructed ending all the progress you've made. If any human being I know is prepared for this, it's you," I said.

"I don't know. Am I? Part of me thinks I'll feel so much better going in there. Meanwhile, the other part of me says jump ship and bail right now," he said rubbing his face vigorously.

"You're ready. Look at Ellie. You really seem happy right now. You're over Callie. You don't think you are one hundred percent over her, but I assure you that you're there, Stone. You're closer than you've ever been. The pain ends after we get this over with. Let's close this book up. It's time," I stated.

"Dammit. I know you're right, you know. I hate it when you're right and I'm not when I so desperately want to be," he smiled halfheartedly chuckling.

"I know Stone. Let me have this one will you?"

"Just this once, man. Let's end this once and for all," he replied. And with that, Alec Stone gathered all the courage he could stir in his haunted heart and set toward the door for the final duel.

***

We took up seating in the back corner on the nice sized wedding chapel. The bridesmaids entered in their lilac gowns,

199

and the groomsmen accompanied in charcoal suits with canary yellow ties. There were white roses wrapped in burlap bouquets and porcelain pearl colored vases throughout the chapel. It was a truly majestic sight. Unlike my normal self, or even most normal men in general, I dreamt of my future wedding. What would it be like? Who would be my best man and groomsmen? Inside or outdoors? Maybe more, who would be standing across from me looking down the one-way tunnel that lasts for all eternity? I hoped she would come soon. Maybe I had already met her. I was never the most patient person.

Suddenly, the organ ricocheted off the walls and the music commenced. Kip strolled down the aisle, seating his grandparents, then Callie's grandparents and then both sets of their parents. He stood handsome, but squirrelly. He was about 5'8 and had curly ringlets of brown hair and a bushy beard that was just slightly lighter in color. He wore a white dress shirt, charcoal slacks, plaid suspenders and a yellow bowtie. The attire felt casual for a wedding, but according to Stone, Callie and Kip were essentially hippies of the modern era. Then, she sauntered from behind the double doors with her father. She looked like a hippie angel, wearing a crown of roses around her head with a casual lace dress that was tight to her neck with eyelets. It had sleeves that were lace and sheer and fell ¾ length on her heavily freckled arms. For all of the things I thought of her and for all the resentment I harbored toward her because of what she had put my best friend through, she looked as lovely as I'd ever seen her.

Stone watched her every step, tracing her flat ballet shoes to her crowned head with familiar glances—the glances of someone who had once loved every inch of her. His eyes were heavy, tears were bubbling beneath his eyes and he was mesmerized. I murmured something, but he did not reply. The girls sat silently and stoic, staring at her as if she held the key to everything good in life the way most brides captivate an audience on their most ceremonious day. She passed us by quickly, staring ahead at the figure of her future. She wept, but controlled, and met Kip at the altar after a tearful kiss and hug from her father. She stood facing us, and in an instance my eyes were seared with fervor. Her eye line met mine, her emerald green eyes shaped like walnuts jumped bewildered at my presence. I smiled and nodded, pursuing my lips as if to tell her I was sorry. I knew it was only a matter of seconds until she noted Alec who was sitting two seats over.

Like a lighthouse guiding a ship toward it in the night, her eyes pulled his into a cataclysmic fusion. Their eyes danced intensely, almost sharing a full conversation while the Preacher began to talk about the importance of faithfulness in marriage. Her eyes darted madly between Alec and Kip. Kip, looking agitated, looked back over his shoulder but did not have an angle to see Stone. Kip noticeably whispered, "You okay?" to Callie and she nodded convincingly. But she continued to look back toward Alec Stone. In those seconds, it was almost as if they were reliving their entire history, each memory a capsule separated into the space of time that could never be taken away. Alec continued nodding and staring into his former lovers eyes through thunderstorm tears and for even one second, I could see a bond in both their eyes. Was she questioning if she was holding hands and uniting futures with the right person? Just as I gave in to the theory that she was doing that exactly, she took her dainty pointer finger and swiped the tears off of her cheeks, and locked her pupils with Kip's. There was no going back for Callie and Alec Stone. Within a burst of minutes that strung together and played out like hours, the newlyweds shared a kiss, to many congratulations. Stone sat with a look of emaciation, albeit temporarily. Callie exited the chapel without another glance at her former lover. She fought her past with all that she was capable of fighting with, and moved on. Exactly the way it's supposed to be. Despite his distraught appearance, the face of a warrior who had fought a long-winded battle, relief set in Alec Stone that it was truly over. Stone had conquered his fear. He had conquered his past. A new sun would arise the next morning and it would be different. Alec's heart had to suffer one last ghastly blow to realize it was undeniably time to heal. Life can be like that. Sometimes it takes one knock out punch, a kick to the stomach, a horrendous fall from grace—to find that we can stand on our own two feet again. God made His people capable and victorious. Sometimes the only thing that can reveal that truth to us is the passing of time. And maybe, in Alec Stone's case, witnessing your truest love more in love with her life than she had ever been prior. Though it's a mystifying lesson, a knife to the heart really, seeing her elation precisely what it took to bury Alec's deep seeded sorrow and resentment. Callie had chosen Kip to spend her life with. Everything was set in stone, clear as crystal; he had no room to influence the situation any longer, nor did she.

As we walked out the chapel that night, I knew Alec Stone was going to see life return the zest he gave to it back to him. Was it with Ellie or someone else altogether? A stranger who we had yet to encounter? That, I did not know yet. I just hoped I would be along for the ride to share in the next excursion under the heavenly spider web skies. For some relationships, we experience ebb and flow, but the truest of counterpoint souls, the souls that understand one another backwards and forwards, whether they are near or far, stay connected one way or another. This was the case with my friend, Alec Stone. Though time and distance would at times attempt to get in the way, our friendship would remain fully in tact. The way it was intended to be all along.

Made in the USA
Lexington, KY
23 June 2015